I0660071

Fountains of Youth

A collection of short stories

By

Rick Elliott

Rising River Press

www.risingriverpress.com

ISBN: 978-0-9846004-1-0

LCCN: 2011913428

Printed in the United States of America

Rising River Press

For Dave—long gone but not forgotten

Stories

♦

Marlena

No doubt about it, Marlena was a tough girl. You'll see what I mean in a minute. Her doe-eyes and honey-colored hair would melt you if she turned her attention your way. And for a seventeen year-old, she was built like a brick shithouse.

We lived in Oakville, a no-stoplight town just down the road from Sheriff Taylor and Mayberry. Our high school class had twenty-two in it. This meant there were no cliques. And despite my being only a quarter-inch away from a hare-lip, I talked to her as much as anyone since I helped her in math class, plus we both worked at the sale barn on Saturdays.

Marlena moved down here two years ago from Kansas City with her mom, step-dad and three young half-siblings. I moved to Oakville when I was nine, straight out of foster care—the result of being signed on as a slave to two, new age, childless, do-gooders with a recently purchased twenty-acre goat and rabbit farm at the edge of town.

"What's it like living in a big city?" I asked her once.

"Ahh, not that much different from here, just more of it, Witt," she answered in a soft, matter-of-fact voice as she stared past me into the distance.

Witt was my nickname, as in Dimwit. When I first moved here, I was so mad at the world I didn't utter a sound for a week at school, and everyone thought I was stupid. Dimwit got shortened to Wit, and it stuck. I added the second "T".

"More of what?" I asked naively, wanting to keep the conversation going.

"More people wanting stuff."

1

"What stuff?"

"Wanting money, wanting to grab your ass or rub against your tits. Of course, none are more persistent than Doyle Perkins on Saturdays," she explained ending with a derisive laugh.

We both ended up at the sale barn; she because her half-siblings had outgrown diapers and her lazy-ass, rarely-employed step-dad told her to go find a job and help chip in with the grocery bills, and me because goat and rabbit hadn't caught on with the taste buds of the local beef eaters.

Minimum wage was a foreign phrase around these parts, especially to the owners of the Perkins Bros. Livestock Auction and Sale Barn. But it was one of the few jobs around, unless you wanted to get up at four a.m. and be a teat-jerker or waste-management specialist on one of the dairy farms dotting the surrounding hills.

Marlena's boyfriend, Russ, made the three hour trip from Kansas City in his souped-up, black Trans Am every Saturday to meet her at the sale barn, having been warned away from the house by her step-dad and the unquestionable barrel of his .38 Special. He was afraid of losing his cheap labor, though he hadn't caught on to their Saturday afternoon rendezvous, yet. It wasn't any of my business, but I kept it in the back of my mind as a trump card. Russ and I weren't always friends. By accident, I got on his hard-to-find good side after fixing the fuel pump in his car one weekend that would have left him stranded in Oakville.

At the sale barn, I sorted calves as they came in, pairing them up with others that matched their sex, size and color before sending the paperwork up to the office. I could write legibly and had a knack for it.

Russ, if he got there in time, would help unload the reluctant pigs and goats from the back of pickup trucks or the occasional car trunk, not because he ever got paid, but because he enjoyed wrestling with them and throwing them around. He called it therapy.

Marlena helped the vet back at the hydraulic squeeze chute. Any cows or bulls that came in had to have blood drawn and tested for Bangs before they could be sold. More than once, I saw her get knocked back ten feet by a pissed-off cow that she got too close to as she tried to put the heavy, chrome-plated, nose grabs in place to pull its head around. She did this so the vet could stick the beast in the jugular vein while Marlena read off the ear tag number for the paperwork. She would give a little embarrassed laugh, work her tongue across her upper teeth with her lips closed to make sure her retainer was still in place, and get right back in there. No matter how much it hurt (and I know it did sometimes), she wasn't about to let the local goobers lined up along the fence watching this free show see her shed a tear.

And what a spectacle the sale barn was, like a carnival, flea market and medicine show all rolled into one. Every six-toed hillbilly in the county showed up on Saturdays to buy or sell something or just to hang around and chew the fat with others of their ilk. With a dribble of brown juice, starting at the corner of their mouth and meandering down their chin, they'd bump the shoulder of some city kid down visiting grandma and grandpa, offering them a wad of Red Man just to watch them run off in disgust, their mouths agape from culture shock. For the natives, I think it was the highpoint of their week.

Castrating pigs was a particularly well-attended event. The vet would do it after they were sold, before the new owner took them home. Sometimes there were shoats pushing a hundredweight. Most hadn't seen a human being since birth until the Friday night before sale day. They'd get trapped up in the wooded slopes behind the house of a cunning, tobacco-chewer, needing to pay this month's bill from the electric co-op. The hayseeds that weren't lucky enough to catch a pig had to take their chances messing with the electric meter attached to the light pole.

When the vet mashed a young boar against the wooden fence to slow him down as the herd raced around in a dizzying circle, Marlena would grab a hind leg. Slick as snot, she'd twist them down onto their side, shoving their head to the ground with her left forearm while simultaneously burying one knee into their ribcage and the other into their gut in front of a hip bone. Marlena would pull the surgical candidate's upper back leg toward its head so as to give the vet a clear shot at the target with his gleaming scalpel blade. She'd hang on for dear life as the pig jerked violently trying to escape her grasp all the while praying the vet wouldn't mistake her white knuckles for the pig's nether parts. Those were the little ones. The big ones she'd lay on while grabbing hold of the board fence to brace herself.

A collective groan would rise up from the crowd gathered around as the mountain oysters were ripped from their porcine owner before being quickly drowned out by a frantic, high-pitched, ear-splitting scream from the offended patient. The next sound was the occasional retching of a weak-stomached soul as the oysters, trailing a thin stream of blood, got tossed over the fence. They'd be caught in mid-flight and swallowed whole by a waiting border collie or blue heeler sidetracked from its duck-herding duties. It never failed that when I happened to be in the vicinity and stopped to watch, I would reflexively cover my crotch and feel a sympathetic, deep pain run up my loins all the way to my gut.

Before the cattle sale started at one o'clock, after the pigs, goats, chickens, ducks, occasional llama, cheap saddles, grass hay and kitchen sinks had been sold, Marlena and I would sit back by the squeeze chute comparing our wounds while eating greasy hamburgers from the sale barn café. Long ago she'd shown me, and me only, the wire retainer and fake front upper tooth. Her "real" dad had knocked the first one out while trying to knock some sense into her when she was eleven.

Once, she unbuttoned the top of her blouse and pulled her bra part way back to show me a greenish-yellow bruise at the base of her left breast, the result of being bit by a mean-ass, two-year old, pinto colt the Saturday before. They had to be bled, too. It seems like everyone had to give blood at this place. I swear I could see the edge of her deep red areola and was caught between fainting and a boner. Luckily, a rogue cow saved me. She'd knocked the gate open in pen thirty-seven and came barreling by us with two pen riders hot on her tail, their horses' shod hooves kicking up sparks on the concrete alleyway. I say lucky because I was mesmerized and came this close to kissing that breast when Russ, decked out in his standard black leather coat and matching fingerless gloves, came shuffling around the corner. She ran to him, gleefully wrapping her arms around his thick neck and kissing him forever. Each time I saw them together like that, the same feeling swept over me as when watching those pigs get their testicles ripped out.

Russ was dumb as a fence post and we got along okay. He didn't perceive me as much of a threat with my looks and me wearing a tattered, feed company-embossed coat, self-repaired with pieces of duct tape placed over the rips and smelling like a billy goat. In fact, he let me chaperone Marlena to a dance one Saturday night when he had to work overtime.

Besides being four years older, Russ worked at a foundry in Kansas City making good money, and every time I got the chance I asked him if the place was hiring. He'd shake his head and give me some lame excuse. But I was persistent, if nothing else, and I kept after him to let me know if he ever got wind of any openings. I even offered to let him stay over at my house (though I hadn't okayed it with the "do-gooders") on a Saturday night hoping Marlena would think better of me. And, thinking too that Russ might return the favor when the time was ripe for me to blow Oakville for a high dollar job in the big city. I found out later the only reason he got the job at the foundry was because his ol' man was some big shot in the local steel workers union.

Marlena told me, more than once, that as soon as she turned eighteen, Russ had a job lined up for her at one of the strip clubs on Independence Street in K.C. making three hundred bucks a night. She would be O...U...T..., out of here. She and Russ were eager for that.

Ever since Marlena confided to me about Doyle Perkin's roaming hands, I tried to stay a little closer to her when we were alone at the back end of the cattle pens. Not because she asked me to, but because, well..., just because. I wanted to ask her—though I never did—why she didn't tell Russ about him, betting Russ would put Doyle in his place. In the end, I figured she needed the money same as me.

Like clockwork, when everyone else was up at the sale ring, Doyle, wearing his felt, "open road" Stetson tilted a little to the side, thumbs hooked over his belt and strutting like a bantam rooster, would show up at the vet chute just as the auctioneer's call for the first pen of calves echoed through the barn. He'd peruse the cow pens, looking for any keepers to take back to the ranch while spelling his name in piss on the dust-covered, rough-hewn, board fence. Next, he'd sidle over close to Marlena under the guise of wanting to see the charts listing the cattle owner's names, putting his arm around her, pulling her real close before telling her, in a joking manner, if she ever got tired of Russ, she knew where to find him. He thought he was slicker than cow's shit after a belly full of late April grass (Marlena's words..., and mine). Then, one Saturday a month before the end of the school year, things came to a head.

There was a clapboard tack room the size of a small garage across from the alleyway leading to the hydraulic squeeze chute. Doyle Perkins and his older brother, Merle, kept all their cattle working supplies inside. Ear tags, emasculators, branding irons, balling guns, dehorners, you name it, if it pertained to cattle, it was in that room.

Marlena was in there putting away the nose grabs when Doyle happened upon her. He was giving her a full body rub while she tried to squeeze past him. I was standing on the catwalk attached to the alleyway opposite the store room, watching Doyle make his move while I half-heartedly scraped back tag glue with a curry comb from the hair of some recent white-faced arrivals. Twice in the past year I'd received an ass-chewing for either not getting the old glue off or not covering it precisely with a new number tag.

"Goddamn it, Witt. Nobody likes to buy a stale road-weary cow," Doyle would growl. Then he'd fly off the handle.

When Russ's Trans Am pulled up in the parking lot, I couldn't decide who to warn. As much as I despised Doyle, I felt like I owed him something. He'd taught me a lot of things since I'd started working here: how to judge livestock, how to fight (he'd boxed competitively during a stint in the army), and how *not* to behave around women.

Russ came around the corner and before he could say a word I nodded towards the tack room. I figured, in the end, neither one of them would help me in a pinch so I stayed neutral, waiting for the fireworks to commence; Oakville entertainment at its finest. Doyle, with his back to the doorway, was trying to persuade Marlena into going out on the town some night.

"What about your wife?" I heard Marlena ask.

"And what about me? You sawed-off runt," Russ shouted, climbing the two wooden steps into the room.

"Well, hello, Russ," Doyle offered with a grin, not easily perturbed.

I got the feeling that Doyle had been caught in this position before—with his pants down (figuratively speaking on this particular day).

Russ was cussing a blue streak, throwing any loose objects he could get his hands on at Doyle as Marlena ducked out the door. Doyle had both arms raised as if he was being held up by a bank robber.

"Now, simmer down, Russell," Doyle admonished, his voice deep and even like he was trying to calm a skittish colt. "I was just having some innocent fun that's all. No need to get all riled up."

"Simmer down, my ass, you son of a bitch."

Russ flung a one pound horn weight that just caught Doyle's hat as he ducked.

"Now, goddamn it, Russ, keep this up and I'll fire your worthless butt and not pay you a red cent."

Well, I can tell you that went over real big with Russ who'd never seen a dime from that tightwad in all the months he'd been coming here, helping out for free. Of course, in their defense, the Perkins brothers weren't dummies. If someone wanted to help for free without being asked, far be it for them to say no.

"How the hell are you gonna fire me when you've never hired me, you sorry piece of trash."

Russ had moved on to the heavy artillery, picking up a broken pistol-grip syringe.

"Now..., now hold on a minute there, son," Doyle offered, never taking his eyes off Russ. "We can remedy that situation right now."

From where I was standing, a little higher than the floor of the shack they were in, I saw Doyle lower his left arm and reach into his pants pocket, pulling out a wad of bills that would choke a draft horse. I watched his other arm moving slowly higher over his head, toward something I couldn't see but I knew whatever it was, it spelled trouble for Russ. Never take your eye off the bull. A lesson taught to me by none other than Mr. Doyle Perkins. But Russ did, reaching down to pick up the one hundred dollar bills as they fluttered to the floor from Doyle's hand.

"That's more like it, you miserable motherf...," was the last statement Russ uttered as Doyle crowned him with one of a half-dozen branding irons hanging from nails along the rafter. Unfortunately for Russ, it was the biggest one. It looked like a billboard when singed into the flank of a cow, and on Russ's head it left a hell of a mark. Damn near cold cocked him.

Russ was on his knees, going in circles with one arm covering his bleeding scalp as Doyle whopped him once more on the shoulder. Then, when Russ was facing the general direction of the open doorway, Doyle planted his boot on Russ's backside sending him tumbling down the steps. Russ was lying sprawled out below me, a dusty, size 10 C, imprinted on the seat of his black denim jeans. Doyle came out after him and now stood next to me though two feet below as I leaned back casually against the steel-sided alleyway, still standing on the catwalk.

What a coincidence; two of my favorite people right here in front of me. Russ—back up on his hands and knees, staring up at me, swaying from side to side, his eyes blurry, drool hanging from the corner of his mouth—looked like a long-in-the-tooth nag that had been rode hard and put up wet. Doyle, with his back to me, looked like Zeus about to toss a thunderbolt as he raised the branding iron overhead with both hands. That's when I made my move. It was my way of paying him back. I mean, otherwise, he might have murdered poor Russ, and then where would we have been?

Due to the high cost of batteries, the Perkins Bros. had invented a hotshot that required none. A 110 volt fence charger, connected to a bare electric wire that ran along the alleyway served the same purpose with a much improved effect. Another wire, looped over the first and threaded through a half-inch diameter, three-foot long piece of PVC pipe that served as an insulating handle made it a semi-mobile, high-powered cattle prod that could be slid along the whole length of the alleyway. I held it in my hand like a hunting rifle pointing the business end away from me toward the low-slung tin roof that covered the cattle pens and alleyway. It would light you up with a stunning jolt that would make you piss your pants if you touched it. Fortunately for Doyle he'd just emptied his bladder in the usual manner minutes before.

When he raised the branding iron to its full height, it was only two inches from the hot wire. Like Cinderella's fairy godmother, I touched the tip of his branding iron with my magic wand. You could see his arms quiver uncontrollably and the muscles in his jaw clench tight. By the time he managed to release his grip on the branding iron, before bellowing a plethora of cuss words and turning to face me, I'd lowered the prod to the floor and was pointing nonchalantly at the hot wire overhead, indicating the cause of his sudden electrification.

With Marlena's help, Russ staggered toward the gate on the other side of the squeeze chute that led out to the parking lot. Wearing knee-high rubber boots that pointed toward her heart-shaped ass and a T-shirt that came to halt just above her beautiful belly button, it was the last time I ever saw her.

Turns out she went straight to Kansas City that very afternoon with Russ and never looked back. I got a dyslexic letter from her a couple months later explaining all this. She thanked me for saving Russ that day at the sale barn. Fat lot of good it did me. Said she was working, making good money but she didn't say where. Said she was hoping to find a day job soon.

I did manage to get out of Oakville, though it took me two more years. Every now and then, I call home (it never seemed like it when I was living there) and talk to the couple that raised me. The last time we spoke, they told me Doyle Perkins had passed on unexpectedly. Seems he stumbled upon an old bull he'd been missing for a couple of days in one of his pastures. The bull had somehow broken a back leg. Now for those of you unfamiliar with this scenario, let me tell you something: There is nothing in this world more dangerous than a hurt bull. I mean think about it. You're a ton of muscle with forty females to screw any time you wish, day or night, and you break your fucking leg. Wouldn't you be pissed? That's how Doyle explained it to me once when a crippled half breed hauled into the sale barn almost nailed me.

"Witt, don't ever take your eye off a bull," he'd scold; or "Boys, don't stare in awe at the size of his scrotum, but don't ever turn your back on a bull either," he'd explain to any newbies just hired.

His brother found Doyle; chest crushed, barely alive, curled up in a thicket of multiflora rose, the bull standing guard ten feet away. I could just picture it: the wild-eyed beast quivering from ears to twitching tail, nostrils flared, his head held high and swinging violently from side to side by the strength of a massive humped neck, searching the air for any unfamiliar scent as it tried in vain to paw the ground with three good legs.

The bull was dispatched with a lever-action .30-.30 Merle kept behind the seat of his pickup for calf-eating coyotes, but Doyle succumbed before reaching the hospital twenty-five miles away.

Down the road, for Marlena's sake, I hope Russ fares better.

Rick Elliott

Billy Boutwell's Revenge

"Fifty-one bottles of beer on the wall! Fifty-one bottles of beer…"

Our revelry ceased as we coasted into the high school parking lot just shy of midnight. There in front of us, ghoulishly illuminated by the pale blue glow of a mercury vapor street light, was Richard Boutwell, Billy's dad, pacing along the edge of the asphalt. He had a menacing look on his stubbled face and what appeared to be a baseball bat in one hand. The meat of it rested on his broad shoulders. His other hand was out of sight behind his back. We'd left Billy behind in this same parking lot some seven hours ago because he was five seconds late.

Corky Schwartz, our interim manager and sporting a massive headache, rolled the beleaguered '65 Fairlane station wagon to a stop beside Richard, oblivious as to why he was standing there. A baseball glove covered with dark splotches and cradling a pair of crushed, black, horn-rimmed glasses materialized in the hand that had been behind his back. The other nine of us, crammed into the overtaxed car, had an inkling of what was coming, and we collectively swallowed hard. Any worries we had of explaining to our parents why we were late getting home from the ballgame evaporated, replaced by a more concrete one staring us in the face.

Our Pony League team, the Ellsworth Eagles, was scheduled to play the second game of a twilight double header against the Carrolton Copperheads in a tournament to determine the league champion. Our one loss during the summer season came two weeks ago; the result of a squibbler that went right between Billy Boutwell's legs at second base allowing the winning runs to score.

Corky, at nineteen and four years our senior, had agreed to take over as coach this week for John Lee who had left on vacation. We figured, after nine weeks of coaching a bunch of hormone-addled fifteen year olds graduating from bubble gum to chewing tobacco, he deserved of a week in the rest home. Mr. Lee had agreed to loan Corky the station wagon—plus cash—after Corky began to have second thoughts about volunteering his time.

All of us, including Billy, had been told through the grapevine (cell phones were still a decade away) to meet in the parking lot at 5:30; although, when asked, Jesse Choate, our conniving third baseman, was somewhat ambiguous as to whether he had told Billy 5:30 or 5:45.

With a full squad of nine and an hour drive ahead of us, we convinced Corky it was time to go. The aging Fairlane sputtered out of the parking lot, engulfed in an oil-burning haze, as Corky leaned over, preoccupied with finding a radio station to his liking. The four of us, wedged at various angles in the back seat along with our gear, saw Billy come running full-tilt around the corner of Maple and Delaware, his over-sized ball glove on one hand repeatedly pushing up at his horn-rimmed, coke-bottle thick glasses while a ball bat in his other hand pumped up and down in unison with his arm. Jesse, his legs hooked over the rear door, gave a nudge that rippled silently through the car like a pebble dropped in a pond. Everyone, save Corky who was pounding on the dash above the radio, turned, looking back toward a red-faced, puffy-cheeked Billy steadily gaining ground on the rolling box turtle of a car.

Jesse, with no dissention from the rest of us, raised his finger to his lips. Edgar Williams, the tallest of us at six feet-two inches, sat in the middle of the second row and, stretching to his full height, blocked the rear view mirror. Randy Mattson, complaining of heat rash near his nether parts and sitting behind Corky, stuck his foot out the window, claiming the rushing air soothed him. Dave Bates, an unnatural left-hander due to an arm crippling, farm machinery accident as an adolescent, who sat in the front seat, stuck his withered, gloved hand out the window, resting it effectively on the passenger side mirror. By the time we reached highway speed at the S-curves and Corky complained about not being able to seeing behind him, Billy was just a tiny, unrecognizable speck in the mirror.

"If he'd run that fast during games, he wouldn't have been zero for eight in stolen base attempts," Randy Mattson snorted.

Most of us, our teenage conscience fading faster than Billy, nodded in agreement. Billy was a thorn in our collective team spirit.

It wasn't that Billy was less skilled than some of the others of our team. It was more the fact that he always wallowed in his own self-pity when he screwed up. I mean jeez, Randy, our center fielder had been diagnosed with a brain tumor six months ago. Despite intermittent double vision that caused him to go after the wrong fly ball more than once, not to mention playing hell with his batting average, he never complained; and the rest of us knew better than to. He was tough.

And Dave, sharing time between first base and the pitcher's mound with Edgar, screwed up more than a blind hunting dog. But, to his credit, he was the most accomplished liar amongst us. If he missed a ball at first base, it was because the sun got in his eyes, or the string on his glove broke, or a girl in the stands winked at him. And, if he struck out swinging on a slow fastball, a foot off the plate, helmet high, it was a result of the home plate umpire farting, causing him to lose his focus or…; the sun was in his eyes. The very same sun that a half-inning earlier, facing the opposite direction caused him to miss a pickoff throw from Edgar. It was never because of his arm, and God-forbid if anyone suggested otherwise. Yes, we admired his skill in the lying department, hoping to emulate him when each of us turned sixteen and acquired our driver's licenses or girlfriends.

Already ten miles from town, with the Fairlane's faded, beige hood pointed skyward at a thirty-degree angle, like an airplane in a perpetual state of taking off, Billy Boutwell had escaped our minds completely. He'd been replaced by Corky Schwartz's lurid details of a recent date with Tonya Larson, a hometown vixen two years older than the rest of us. By coincidence, this revelation was followed by Jeff Reese, our catcher, pointing at a fat Angus bull blissfully servicing a white face heifer along the fence next to the highway. After a round of spittle-producing laughter and the simultaneous readjusting of our crotches, we got down to the business at hand: how we were going to pulverize the Carrolton Copperheads.

Edgar, our flame-throwing ace, read off the batting averages of our opponents along with a brief scouting report produced by Coach Lee during the last game we'd played against them. The one Billy Boutwell had let slip between his legs. Whatever comment Coach scribbled next to Billy's error on the scorecard had been dutifully and heavily scratched out. Pieces of lead from a #2 pencil were embedded in the thick paper of the scorecard.

At our golden age, between puberty and parenthood, we still believed in omens. And, if not for Corky Schwartz, a second-year college boy majoring in Zoology, raining on our parade, it would have been a good one. Because just as we crossed the bridge over Lake Ellsworth, an eagle flew across the highway in front of us not thirty feet off the ground, struggling to gain altitude while a writhing copperhead gripped in its talons bounced like a spring with each thrust of its outstretched wings. We were slack-jawed in awe of this good luck sign, our confidence miraculously buoyed until Professor Schwartz pointed out that it wasn't an eagle at all but instead a chicken hawk and the snake, a common corn snake not a copperhead.

Oh, well. With that vision shattered, we turned our imaginations to hoisting the league trophy overhead, along with a bound and gagged Corky Schwartz, before tying them both to the chrome luggage rack of the station wagon and driving ourselves to a national title game.

The third-place game, a knuckle biter, went into extra innings, which meant our game started an hour late. That, coupled with the fact that Corky decided to have Dave Bates be our starting pitcher were the reasons we were so late getting home to the pacing Richard Boutwell and the fate that awaited us.

Edgar, a no-nonsense, hard-throwing right-hander with good control, had pitched two days ago and our interim manager figured his arm to be a little tired. When Edgar pitched, the game rarely lasted more than two hours. When Dave pitched, they outlasted a graduation ceremony.

This was the result of Dave being an unnatural lefty. Natural lefties, for whatever reason, tend to be a little wild. Unnatural lefties make a shotgun pattern look tight at a hundred yards. Dave walked one or two per inning with the occasional hit batsman. To his credit, he made this work to his advantage; at least that's what he told us. The batters were swinging as wildly as the pitches he threw. It was a defense mechanism to avoid being hit. Then, when Dave's arm began to play out in the late innings, Edgar would be summoned in from first base to mow down the opposing batters in short order—worn out from defending themselves against Dave. This strategy had worked before and tonight was no exception.

With the championship trophy in hand and Corky behind the wheel, we stopped at a Dairy Queen in Carrolton putting the owners over the top financially for the year and putting a severe dent in Coach Lee's post-game refreshment budget, which had been foolishly entrusted to Corky Schwartz.

The furthest thing from our mind on the way home was Billy Boutwell as we relived every inning of the championship game after which Jeff Reese led us in a bawdy rendition of "Ninety-Nine Bottles of Beer". Further away still was Billy's dad, Richard.

With the Fairlane's engine off, the parking lot was eerily quiet. The only sounds were the irregular ticking metal of the cooling engine, the hum of the pole light, and the low, measured voice of Richard Boutwell. It was like the warning rumble from a volcano as he leaned down toward the open window next to Corky. In the semi-darkness we could see his cheeks sucking in and out and the blood pulsing in his neck veins. Then he erupted.

Poor Corky; he was taking the brunt of Richard's verbal abuse without even knowing why which made up for him dashing our hopes when crossing Lake Ellsworth earlier.

From the back seat, Jeff Reese (his dad had served in the navy) whispered, "He's madder than a sailor with a limp dick in a whorehouse."

Those of us that heard him were pinching ourselves trying not to laugh which would have been our death knell the way Mr. Boutwell was tapping that bat on the roof of the car. Then Randy Mattson spoke up.

"We had to be there by seven o'clock or else we would've had to forfeit the game," Randy said, offering up the trophy in Richard Boutwell's direction.

"I saw someone come around the corner as we were leaving but, from the distance, I thought it was a jogger," Dave Bates offered. "And we needed to get to the game and back in time for Randy's medication," he added somberly, his voice trailing off for effect.

Damn he was good!

Mr. Boutwell, though still livid, had cooled down from white-hot to dull red.

With just a smidgen of a guilty conscience, Jesse Choate, upon close inspection of the crushed glasses and the ball glove that appeared to be smeared with dried blood, inquired about Billy. All of us held our breath, fearing the worst.

Turns out, he was so pissed off at us, he swung his ball bat against a school bus tire in the parking lot, and the bat ricocheted back smashing him in the face. His busted glasses had fallen off his bloodied nose and he'd stepped on them according to Mr. Boutwell.

Everyone in the Fairlane, besides Corky, who was rubbing his temples, breathed a sigh of relief. Because Billy wasn't dead; or because we'd left him behind and won the championship game? No fifteen-year old in the car was ready to wrestle with that moral dilemma.

The next day we apologized to Billy and let him keep the trophy until Coach Lee got back from vacation. The next year, Billy became our starting centerfielder with the explicit instructions that under no circumstance was he to ever attempt stealing a base. It was Randy Mattson's last request.

Rick Elliott

Mr. Propane

Jenny Martens moved her petite frame briskly. Her high heels tapped against the tile floor as she carried a pitcher of water from the stained enamel sink against the far wall over to the coffee pot sitting on its own cart beside her overflowing secretary's desk. The coffee pot began to sputter as cars and trucks rumbled by on Maple Street. The cuckoo clock mounted on the wall, a gift to the owner of the business, signaled the eight o'clock hour and the start of another business day at Tri-county Propane, one block off the square, in Willow Brook, the county seat.

"Morning, Jenny," Bill Dennison grumbled, stepping through the front door of Tri-County Propane.

"Good morning, Bill. Are you ready for a busy day?"

"Do I have a choice? It's supposed to get colder than a witch's tit in a brass bra tonight. We'll be up half the night filling propane tanks for all the damn procrastinators."

"William Dennison, you watch your mouth," Jenny admonished, standing with her hands akimbo, a stern look on her face, "or else I'll call Dorothy and tell her to send you to bed without supper tonight."

"Hah, some threat that is," Bill countered in his booming voice. He removed his ball cap with the company logo on it and ran his thick fingers through his matted hair. "I'll be too busy to get anything but a sandwich for supper tonight. Why does everyone have to wait until the first cold snap to get their tanks filled?"

"It's the nature of the human race, Bill. Everyone hopes it won't get cold; that we'll have a mild winter and they won't have a heating bill to pay," Jenny countered, knowingly.

21

She lit her second cigarette of the morning from the remnants of the first one, avoiding the lipstick ringing the filter as she held it pinched between her polished fingernails. The polish matched her lipstick, shoes and belt that hung just above her hips as an accessory to her fashionable dress.

"Now, you're right about that last part," Bill agreed, pointing toward Jenny. "It's the deadbeats that wait 'til the last minute to call in asking to have their tanks filled. I'll bet nine times out of ten they're the ones that phone in an order at the last minute when they're already out of gas and the weatherman on Channel 7 has been warning for three days that the temperature is going to drop like a rock."

Jenny exhaled, blowing a ring of smoke from her pursed lips as she leaned back in her creaking wooden chair.

"You're all heart, Bill. Where's your compassion, your sympathy for the poor?"

Bill groused, "You sound like that guy, what's his name, there in the paper, that's running for president."

He gestured toward the morning paper unfolded atop stacks of receipts and invoices engulfing the surface of her desk.

"Him?" she asked, pointing at the candidate's picture gracing the front page.

"Yeah, him. I watched him on TV the other night. According to him, if we hug each other a little more, all our problems will be solved, even the deficit."

Jenny studied the picture, "Hmmm…, he can hug me any time. I think he's kind of cute."

Bill waved her off.

"Geez, it's not a beauty contest for cryin' out loud. It's the leader of the free world we'll be voting for next month."

Jenny ignored his comment with a shrug of her shoulders as she began the task of sorting through yesterday's paperwork brought in the previous evening by the delivery truck drivers after the office had closed for the day.

"Is the big guy in yet?" Bill asked, moving toward the door that led into another room at the end of this larger one. It was a small office used by the owner of the company.

"No, he phoned in just before you got here," Jenny answered.

"And?"

"And nothing. He was checking to see if you were late getting to work again this morning is all."

"Oh, that's a bunch of bull! What do you mean…, late again? I'm never late," he huffed.

Bill's face turned red. He prided himself on being punctual. It irritated him to no end that some of the drivers were always late getting in of a morning. They were always taking long lunch breaks or cutting out early on slow days if the boss wasn't around, despite having tanks in need of repair or maintenance work to do on the delivery trucks.

The work ethic of the younger drivers was horrendous he always told Dorothy, his wife of thirty-four and three-quarter years, at the dinner table when the conversation came around to how his work day had been. One driver in particular, Jake Young, who seemed to do no wrong in anyone else's eyes, especially Jenny Martens' or the boss's, always got him worked up.

Jenny laughed; a raspy laugh that indicated how long she'd been smoking Virginia Slim Menthols.

"Relax Bill, I was just funnin' ya. Calm yourself or you'll have another heart attack."

"Okay, okay, very funny. And what about the big guy?"

"He said he'd be a little late getting in this morning. He was going to check on a tank that might be leaking and then he was going to try to collect on a couple of overdue bills. By the way, did you turn your tickets in from yesterday?"

Bill patted the front of his new, scarlet-colored jacket with Tri-County Propane embossed in gold stitching on the back then reached for an inner pocket that contained his bundle of tickets.

"Boy, I almost forgot these, sorry about that," he offered directing the bundle of yellow papers toward Jenny's outstretched arm.

"Uh huh, you know what they say, it's the mind that goes first," she joked, staring into his dark eyes.

At the last second, he jerked the tickets back just beyond her reach. She leaned further across the desk and grabbed at them again. On the third try, she snatched them from his hand only to lose her balance and fall against the top of her desk, face down, her forearms hanging over the front side, tickets in hand, her legs dangling from the opposite side of the desk with the tips of her patent leather shoes just touching the tile floor in front of her chair.

Bill laughed. "Now that's a compromising position to be in."

"Oh Bill, you're such a flirt," Jenny rebuked, feigning disgust as she rearranged her dress and sat back down in her chair.

"By the way, what's the name of that perfume you're wearing?"

"Now Bill, I'm sure Dorothy already has her own brand of perfume that she, and you, like, so don't go getting any ideas about changing it."

"I'm just asking what the name of it is, that's all. With you smoking like a chimney, I normally can't smell anything, but this morning for some reason I can; or maybe you opened a new bottle of air freshener."

Jenny frowned while staring over the top of her reading glasses at Bill who was perusing the log of today's scheduled deliveries. They were already spilling onto the bottom of the page where the last time printed on the margin said six o'clock.

"It's 'Charlie'."

"Hmm, Charlie who?"

Bill was already lost in thoughts of what route to take in order to get the most stops with the least amount of driving which in turn would get him home the fastest tonight as he'd promised his grandson.

"What?" Jenny said sounding confused as she wrinkled her nose and eye brows.

"Charlie who?" Bill said louder this time, looking up from the logbook toward Jenny.

She shook her head slowly, "Bill, I'm sad to say it, but you're a lost cause."

"Why? What's wrong now?" Bill queried with a look of bewilderment on his face. "Which Charlie are you babbling about? How am I supposed to know? Just because I'm ten years older than you doesn't mean I can't hear. Quit your mumbling."

Jenny let out an audible sigh, removing her glasses and letting them fall onto her chest, held there by a gold chain that disappeared beneath her wavy auburn hair at the back of her neck.

"You asked me what the name of my perfume is," she stated with a note of exasperation in her voice.

"Yeah, so?"

"It's 'Charlie'. The...name...of...my...perfume...is... 'Charlie'.

Jenny spoke these words at a slow, deliberate pace, leaning further forward in her chair with each word, her hazel eyes fixed on Bill, ending with a finality of open-mouthed amazement, her arms and hands raised heavenward as if seeking divine guidance from a deity above.

Bill stood there motionless for just an instant, sorting through in his mind parts of the conversation he'd apparently missed.

"Your perfume is called Charlie?"

"Bingo!"

"Well, that's a silly name for a perfume. Hell, why not call it Davey or Joey or maybe even a woman's name, you know. Wouldn't that make more sense?"

Jenny Martens dropped her arms onto her desk, shaking her head in disbelief as sunlight streaming through the windows reflected off her glasses.

"Don't you have tanks to fill, to move, to repair or replace?"

"Well, yes ma'am I do. And if you'll quit bugging me about the silly name of your perfume, I'll try to finish figuring out my route for today."

Jenny, ignoring his harangue, returned to the task of posting accounts receivable, normally a two hour job but, because of the cold snap, at least a three hour task today. Her concentration was broken by the clank of a brass cowbell hanging just above the front door that sounded off each time it was opened. This time it was Bob Tisdale, the owner of the business, bustling through the doorway and around to the backside of the high countertop, a kind of barrier where customers came to pay their bills.

Bob Tisdale, a ruddy-faced man of forty-nine, had owned Tri-County Propane for the past eleven years, half the number of years that Bill Dennison had worked there. Both men and two generations of their ancestors had lived in or around Willow Brook all of their lives. Having played varsity football and basketball on championship teams at Willow Brook High, then working for several years at the local lumber mill before purchasing the propane business from his wife's childless Aunt and Uncle, Bob Tisdale was well-known and well-liked around the area, all factors that had helped the business prosper.

"Good morning, Jenny. Hey, Bill," Bob greeted while setting another stack of receipts on his secretary's desk. Both returned his greeting.

"Hey, Jenny, can you do me a favor and get out John Goble's statement. He cornered me outside in the parking lot just now, and if he hadn't forgot his checkbook back in his pickup, I'd still be out there jawing with him about the low price of cattle and the high cost of cattle feed while we both froze to death. I've got to get on the phone to the gas distribution center and see when our next shipment is going to get here. You know John, he'll talk my ear off for another hour if I don't go hide in my office."

"Will do," Jenny replied, hopping up from her chair and heading for the file cabinet containing customer's posted accounts.

Bob was not yet willing to join the computer world. "That's why I have you" was always his pat answer when Jenny broached the subject.

"Thanks Jenny, you're an angel. Say Bill, have you been by the nurse tank this morning?" Bob was speaking in his usual, rapid-fire manner as he reached the door to his office.

"Yes, sir, I just came from there. Topped off my truck before heading in here."

"You think there's enough propane in the tank to get us through today if the transport truck doesn't get here from Oklahoma?"

Bob was already at his desk, thumbing through his tattered rolodex for Mid-Continent Wholesaler's phone number as Bill entered, grimacing.

"Boy, it'll be tight if we have a big run today. Hopefully, the other three trucks are already full this morning since the level in the nurse tank is way down from where it was last night when I was out there.

This morning, the lock for the transfer pump was lying on the ground pretty as you please next to the pump when I got there."

"Were the gates locked? Man, I hope they're on their way," Bob wished out loud while he dialed the found number.

"Well, yeah it was locked. But still, they need to lock the pump up too, or someone could climb the fence with a twenty pound tank or…"

Bob raised his hand toward Bill as he leaned back in his chair, phone in hand.

"Hey, this is Bob Tisdale, up at Tri-County Propane in Willow Brook. I wanted to verify a shipment of propane is coming my way today. Yes ma'am, I can hold."

Bill resumed, "...or they could burrow under the fence and hook up a hose to the pump."

"Now Bill, quit looking on the dark side. Jake or Isaac just forgot to lock it most likely. At least they locked the gates. We don't want to make it too easy for the criminal elements around here. We'll have to remind them to lock up. Jake must have been working late last night. He's a go-getter isn't he?"

"Oh, yeah, he does alright," Bill offered flatly, thinking, what's this "we" crap. "But..."

"Hey, that jacket looks good on you," Bob interrupted, "so you were out at the nurse tank last night and this morning, too?"

"You bet. I filled my tank truck last night on my way home around six o'clock. After supper, Dorothy and I went to church, and, can you believe it, two people stopped me after the service was over, before I even shook hands with Reverend Walters, asking if I could fill their tanks today. So I got up early, knowing we probably had a full day on the books already from all the procrastinators, and filled their tanks. I stopped back by the main tank and topped off my truck before heading into the office. That's when I noticed the lock on the ground by the pump."

Bob clapped his hands and rubbed them briskly together, like a dice shooter who just hit their point, as he held the phone against his ear with a scrunched up shoulder.

"Damn it to Hell, that's what I love about this business; sometimes we're in greater demand than the Big Man upstairs."

Bill rolled his eyes and started to protest, but Bob cut him off with another wave of his hand, "Hey, this is Bob Tisdale at Tri-county Propane. How's the weather down..."

Bill waited a moment then stepped out of the tiny office, closing the door behind him, not wanting to listen to the shrill voice of his boss while he finagled another load of gas from the wholesaler. He waved at John Goble, a talkative, widowed rancher from east of town, who was walking out the door to the tune of the tinny cow bell.

Bill grabbed a piece of paper and pen off Jenny Martens' desk and wrote down the names and addresses of today's route. He wanted to get on the road before those jokers, Jake and Isaac, showed up. If things went smoothly today, he might get home in time this evening to make it to his only grandchild's Mighty Mites football game. It was the least he could do for the little fellow since his dad was nowhere to be found anymore. Still, he needed to talk to Bob about taking some vacation time so he and Dorothy could go on a promised cruise for their anniversary; vacation time he didn't have since using it up last year during his recovery from by-pass surgery, not to mention money he didn't have since paying for the operation.

Bob was jabbering away on the phone when Bill finished his route schedule for the day and marked those names off the book. He decided to wait a couple more minutes before starting his route, hoping Bob would be off the phone, determined to ask for some vacation time even if it meant working a few extra weekends.

Glancing at the mirror on the wall, Bill saw himself: fifty-two and already a bum heart despite the doctor's insistence he was as good as new (isn't that what they have to say?); crow's-feet spreading from the corners of his eyes, like pond ice cracking under the weight of a hesitant foot; verging on insolvency due to the medical bills. Yet, physically, he still looked good, didn't he? Still had all of his thick, black hair, could still fit into the same suit he'd owned for thirty-five years, albeit a size tall, extra-large. He knew many locals older than himself, most in worse shape: either overweight, chronic smokers or heavy drinkers whose tickers were still merrily humming along. Where was the justice in that?

Bill could make out snippets of Bob's phone conversation through the closed door. When Bob got excited or agitated, his normal voice, already higher than most men's, bumped up an octave. Though Bob was a star athlete in his younger days, Bill thought him effeminate, not just because of his voice, but because he didn't like to hunt or fish; mainstays, to Bill's way of thinking, in a man's life. Perhaps it was Bob's three daughters who had changed him.

Bill, with his own divorced daughter living back at home and his son now gone, managing a ranch in Colorado, could attest to the fact that with no other male around the house, he himself usually suffered at the whims of the females under roof. No camaraderie about past great hunting seasons, incredible summer fishing trips, or good hay crop years; only talk of recipes and weddings, recitals and child rearing, lousy husbands and occasional tears.

Bill often wondered these days if his life would have been different if he'd had the gumption to buy the propane business from Buck and Faye Haberson, back before Bob fell into it by marrying Linda, their only niece. Would he still be living in his mom and dad's updated old farm house, left to Bill when they passed on? Or would he have a brand new six thousand square foot monster like Bob's, complete with heated pool for spring and fall plus a heated driveway to melt winter's ice and snow? Would he still be driving a Ford Taurus in need of new tires, or would he have a Cadillac with only four thousand miles on it, like Bob Tisdale?

"Are you gonna stand there all day or are gonna deliver some gas?" Bill heard a voice chastising him from behind, followed by a trio of boisterous laughs.

He snapped his head around like a hound after a hungry flea just in time to see Jake, Isaac and Jenny slapping each other on the back as their laughter subsided.

"What were you staring at there, big boy?" Jake asked as he put his hand on Bill's broad shoulder, giving it a squeeze.

"I wasn't staring. I was just thinking about today's route," Bill replied, shrugging off Jake's hand.

"Well, you better quit. It looked painful. Leave the thinking to Bob in there. That's why he gets paid the big bucks," Isaac offered.

"You know, you two are a couple of comedians. With your talent, you ought to be on stage," Bill replied, pausing.

"The first one out of town," the three men said in unison.

"Here, Bill, take this," Jake said with a smile as he held out a five dollar bill, "and go buy yourself a new joke book."

Bill snatched at the money with his left hand as Jake pulled it back.

"Just kidding, big boy, just kidding," Jake cackled.

Jenny had her hand over her mouth, trying not to laugh. "You two are terrible, picking on poor ol' Bill."

"Poor ol' Bill, poor ol' Bill, he sleeps on a mattress stuffed with C-notes and could whip us both with one hand," Isaac countered.

"I could and I should," Bill replied, cracking his knuckles. "Which donut shop have you two been hiding in this morning?"

"Hiding! No way," Jake retorted, a mock look of hurt on his face. "We've been out working this morning, already. You're the one standing here in this nice, warm, cozy office with this good-looking gal, primping yourself in the mirror. What, are you going on a date or something?"

Jake put his arm around Jenny. "How's my girl, Jenny, anyway? Watching Bill there mesmerized by his own reflection, I almost forgot to give you your morning hug."

Bill waved off this last comment and stalked toward the door, grabbing a pair of heavy leather gloves from a shelf behind the counter on his way out.

"I'm doing just fine, thank-you," Jenny answered.

"Say, Bill, you still want to sell that recurve bow?" Isaac shouted after him as he opened the door. He hoped to land a bargain before the start of archery season in two weeks.

Bill stuck his head back in the door and with a smug look on his face replied, "Isaac, it takes a man to handle a fifty pound bow."

"Well, hey, you better sell it to me then," Jake cut in.

"I'd feel guilty selling it to either one of you guys. The deer would laugh themselves to death watching you try to string it," Bill explained.

With that said, Bill headed for his delivery truck content that he'd gotten the last word in against those two slackers.

"Bill's in a sour mood this morning, isn't he?" Jake said to no one in particular.

"I think it made him mad when we finished the punch line of his joke," Isaac surmised.

"Well, I offered him five bucks to go buy a new one, didn't I? He never has liked me anyway. I think he's jealous of my good looks and affable nature."

Isaac scoffed as he ran his finger down the logbook of to-day's delivery schedule. Jake stared into the mirror, mocking the now absent Bill as he combed his hair.

"What do you think, Jenny? Aren't I better looking than ol' Bill?" Jake inquired, tilting the mirror just enough to see Jenny's reflection in it.

"Mmmm, I don't know," Jenny considered as she placed a finger on her lips in contemplation.

Jenny Martens, a divorced mother of two teenage daughters, still hoping, arguably with a few good years left in her, for the right man to come along, knew how Jake looked better than she cared to admit. Jake had moved fast when he first came to Willow Brook five years ago and began working at Tri-County Propane. He liked to party, as did Jenny, liked to throw some money around on his girl unlike Jenny's first husband, a tightwad except when it came to booze and card games.

Once Jake found out she had two kids to feed, the party ended between them as quickly as it had started. She'd found out that offspring were a liability with most of the men she dated since her divorce, not just Jake. At least Jake made her laugh here at the office. Still, he could be full of himself sometimes, she thought. What she wanted more than anything right now in her life was stability, reliability, a man with a steady paycheck wouldn't hurt either; someone like Bob Tisdale or Bill, only younger.

Bill took off in his delivery truck heading west on Route 62, still agitated by those two, Jake and Isaac. "Just ignore them," Dorothy always told him over dinner when their talk at the table turned to his job. Easy for her to say, he thought, she didn't have to listen to those smart alecks every day. No way was he selling his prize bow to either of them. Besides, he might keep it to hunt this year, what with ammunition so high. He could find something else to sell if need be to help pay for the cruise. It was a promise he now regretted but knew from the look on Dorothy's face when he'd made it that she would be terribly disappointed if he reneged.

Driving along the ridges that the highway followed afforded Bill a front row seat as autumn displayed its latest offering of colors. The view was not likely to last much longer. With the temperature already dropping, the change in the weather brought strong winds that would coax the remaining foliage into letting go, leaving the trees stripped and bare until spring.

His first stop was at a dairy three miles off the two-lane highway. By the time he'd filled the tank and gabbed for a moment with the owner of the farm, Jack Wallace, about the abundant crop of acorns, a fall staple for deer and turkey, and what it meant to the upcoming hunting season, a half hour had passed. Bill was already glancing at his watch, calculating how long it might take him to finish at his next stop.

By early afternoon, Bill had made six stops to fill tanks before he pulled into the gravel parking lot of the Lakeview Café, a nondescript-looking diner with an adjacent bait shop that, in Bill's mind, had the best scenery to observe through the windows, not to mention the best fried catfish for lunch.

He wasn't slacking off since the business was on his list of deliveries for the today, something Jake would surely accuse him of if he knew. Chocking the back wheels of the truck, parked on the only level part of the lot, Bill Dennison, having forgotten this morning's irritants, stepped to the edge of the plateau on which the café was situated. He took in the vista spreading out westward before his eyes. The lake, with all its fingers of crooked coves and jagged shoreline, meandered below him, shimmering in a mellow fall sun that was about to be overtaken by an ominous, dark wall of clouds sweeping in from the northwest, pushing the blue sky away to the east.

A dozen species of trees ranging in colors from the brilliant orange of majestic sugar maples to the dull green of scraggly red cedars framed the lake from the surrounding hills that went on endlessly undulating toward the horizon. He took in a deep breath and with it, the unmistakable smells of fall: crisp-drying leaves, mellow hardwood smoke and pungent brown pine needles blanketing one end of the parking lot. At least the seasons still change in a predictable way, Bill thought, heading toward the café entrance.

"Howdy, Bill," Sam Simmons, the proprietor, cried out from behind the counter over the whir of a blender. "Did you bring me some propane?"

"You bet, Sam," Bill answered while waving to acknowledge a few of the other patrons, mostly ranchers and retirees, which he recognized. "Are you getting low?"

"I looked at the gauge yesterday afternoon. It was under ten percent so I thought I better give you guys a call," Sam explained as he set a couple of bowls of steaming chili in front of two customers seated on stools at the counter.

Bill found an empty table by the west-facing windows. He pulled out his delivery list and his cell phone, the one piece of modern equipment Bob Tisdale had sprung for, knowing it would save on miles driven by his trucks. Before he could dial the office, the lone waitress, a quiet, big-boned girl of twenty, poured him a cup of coffee and took his order: the day's special, fried catfish, fresh from a neighbor's commercial raising pond.

"This is your last chance to order catfish for a while," the waitress informed him.

"Oh yeah, why is that?" Bill asked, surprised as much by the fact that the waitress had spoken a full sentence to him as to the content of the sentence. "Is Joe Hamilton going on vacation or something?"

"No, he said the blue herons have nearly wiped out his stocked ponds. Sounds like he ought to shoot'em," she offered.

"Those greedy damn birds," Bill proclaimed, shaking his head, "I'll bet Joe's about to blow a gasket over them, and, by the way, he can't shoot'em because they're a protected species."

The waitress, coffee pot in hand, moved off to another of the eight tables. Bill watched as her long ponytail swayed to and fro in rhythm with her hips. He commenced to dial the office number while glancing at the list of names still to go on his delivery route.

"Tri-County Propane," the cheery voice of Jenny Martens announced over the phone.

"Hey, Miss Sunshine, it's me, Bill. I was just checking in to see if there are any more deliveries I need to make."

Bill said this with his fingers crossed, hoping the answer was no.

"Afraid so, Bill. I've got a couple more for you. Hang on while I go get the logbook."

"Can't Jake or Isaac take care of them," Bill shouted into the phone, forgetting where he was at.

There was no response from the other end of the line. He glanced around the diner to see if he'd embarrassed himself, but no one appeared to be paying him any mind. Through the receiver, he could hear the sound of Jenny's shoes tapping on the floor and muffled voices in the background, probably one of those loafers, Jake or Isaac, he figured.

Jenny's voice came back on the line, "Okay, Bill. Are you ready with a pen and paper? Better write these down so you don't forget them."

"Very funny," he snorted into the phone. "Can't Jake or Isaac take care of them?"

"Isaac has already got deliveries that will keep him out past your bedtime, and Jake has an appointment he says he has to keep at six-thirty tonight," Jenny explained. "And, as Bob pointed out, remember Bob the owner, both addresses are further west of your last delivery so you are the man."

"Well, your lover boy picked a fine time to have an appointment," Bill chided.

"He is not my lover boy. Don't go getting ugly with me, Bill Dennison," Jenny huffed. "Now, take down these names and addresses."

"Hold on a second. Let me get an ink pen," he groused, reaching for a pen in his coat pocket. "Okay, go ahead."

"Terry at K-9 Kennels called and said he needs their tank filled. And Beth Huffman wants a hundred gallons in her little tank. By the way, she's a 'cash only' customer according to our records, so make sure she pays," Jenny informed him.

"Well, that's just great. Now, I have to do Bob's job, too." Bill was trying to keep his voice down. "Did you tell her when she phoned in the order she would have to pay in cash on delivery?"

The question was met with silence on the other end, giving Bill the answer.

"Thanks a lot, Jenny," Bill said with as much sarcasm as he could muster.

"Oh, by the way, Dorothy called and said your grandson's football game was cancelled because of the weather. She said to tell you no one would be home tonight as they were going shopping but not to worry about getting home because she and your daughter had taken care of the livestock. So go out there and earn some money for Tri-County, Bill," Jenny commanded, sounding like a cheerleader.

"Geez, maybe I'll just stay out all night so I can get an early start on tomorrow."

Jenny teased, "That's the spirit, Bill; make Tri-County Propane proud of you. Oh, the other line is ringing. Gotta go. Goodbye."

Sam Simmons brought out Bill's lunch just as he set the phone down hard on the table, shaking his head.

"Having a busy day, Bill?" Sam queried, wiping his hands on his stained, white apron.

"Ah, nothing out of the ordinary, I guess. All the last-minute deadbeats are calling in, demanding that we hurry up and get their tanks filled," Bill said, stuffing a fork full of food in his mouth.

Sam was wringing his apron with his hands, a nervous habit of his, as he spoke in response to Bill's gruff statement, "I would have called sooner but it just slipped my mind."

"No, no Sam, I didn't mean you. Heck, you're a regular customer." Bill paused and wiped his mouth with a napkin from the dispenser on the table that was covered with a checkerboard-patterned oil cloth before changing the subject. "Is anybody catching any fish on the lake today?"

"Those two fellas sitting there," Sam pointed toward the counter stools, "just came in off the lake."

Sam Simmons moved over and sat down on the last stool at the counter and addressed the two fishermen, "What did you guys say you caught out on the lake today?"

The closer of the two answered, "We snagged our limit of walleye after just three hours on the water. Man, they were biting like crazy this morning."

His partner nodded in agreement, adding, "We couldn't keep the bait on the hooks they were hittin' so fast; must be the change in the weather that's coming."

"Maybe you ought to hire these two guys to supply you with fresh fish, Sam," Bill joked. "Sounds like you're not going to be getting anything out of Joe's catfish ponds for a while."

Sam laughed, heading back around the end of the counter to fetch a few more plates the cook had placed upon the window shelf that separated the kitchen from the rest of the café.

"Is that your Nitro fishing boat out there in the parking lot?" Bill inquired of the two fishermen.

"Yep, it sure is," one of them answered.

"It's a nice looking boat. That engine ought to get you around the lake in a hurry," he complemented, referring to the two hundred horse power Mercury outboard.

"Well, thank you. I've been pleased with it so far," the one with the khaki fishing vest answered.

Sam, walking by, interrupted, "What did you do with your boat, Bill?"

"Ah, I had to sell it a couple of months ago to pay some medical bills."

"Well, that's a damn cryin' shame," Sam offered, "That was a nice looking boat."

"Yeah, it was just like theirs," Bill said, pointing toward the two men at the counter. He waved off a refill as the waitress walked by. "I just had a one-seventy-five Merc on mine, but it did the trick."

The fishermen nodded in understanding.

Bill ate the rest of his meal in silence, thinking about his old boat and all the fishing trips he'd taken with his boy, Scott, or some of his friends, including Sam.

The solid waitress brought Bill's check by, dropping it on the table as she headed for another table filled with recent arrivals.

"Well, men, did that chili hit the spot?" Sam asked.

Both fishermen nodded their approval as they got up to leave.

"You fellas come back next time you're out this way," Sam offered as he stepped over to Bill's table and grabbed the check as Bill was about to look at it.

"It's on the house today, Bill. I appreciate you getting by before I ran out of gas."

"You don't have to do that, Sam," Bill protested as he got up from the table.

"Nope, I insist. Uh, if it's okay, just have them send me an invoice for the propane, and I'll get you paid."

"Sure, Bob Tisdale's got enough money to carry us all 'til the end of the month," Bill stated matter-of-factly, starting for the door before turning back to leave a two dollar tip on the table.

"So long, Sam."

"See you later, Bill. Don't be a stranger," Sam admonished from behind the counter where he was busy cutting a fresh pecan pie into slices.

Just as Bill opened the door to leave, Coy Albers, a local stockman and member of Bill's church sauntered into the café.

"Say, Bill, how's it going?" Coy greeted him in his usual slow drawl, not really a southern drawl since technically this was still part of the Midwest. No, it was more of an I'm-never-in-a-hurry-to-do-anything-including-talk kind of drawl.

"Pretty good," Bill replied. "How 'bout yourself?"

"Oh, fair to middlin'," Coy answered. "I thought I'd stop in for some grub before heading over to check on some cows I've got on a rented pasture south of here. Ol' Dorothy was telling me all about you taking her on a cruise for your anniversary at church the other day. She sounded pretty excited."

"Well, I'm glad one of us is," Bill interjected.

Coy chuckled, "You know you're setting a bad example for all of us land-lubbers out here in the countryside. If my wife gets wind of this, no tellin' where I'll have to take her when our time comes."

"Sorry about that, Coy. I guess I'm going to have to learn to keep my mouth shut."

"Yep," Coy agreed, nodding his head slowly. "Say, by the way, since you're out this way, could you stop by and fill my tank. I ain't for sure, but I think it might be getting a little low...."

Bill, with a scowl on his face, started to answer but Coy wasn't finished.

"...as a favor to me. I would surely appreciate it, and I know the Mrs. would, too. Why, if we ran out of gas for the furnace, she might have to go chop wood."

Bill shut his mouth without uttering a word. He just nodded, patted Coy on the shoulder and headed for his truck.

Bill Dennison resigned himself to the fact that he still had a long day ahead of him, but at least there was no rush to get home. And no need to take a break in the evening and drive back to town; all the way to the playing field at Willow Brook Junior High for a chance to watch his grandson play on the football team. He felt obligated to go to the games since the team was sponsored by Tri-County Propane and two other local businesses Bill had cajoled into donating money in return for advertising logos on their jerseys.

With no need to hurry and only one minor worry, hassling Beth Huffman over her payment, the remainder of the afternoon and early evening went by pleasantly for Bill. He marveled at the happiness he felt when no obligations were close on the horizon other than what his work specifically required. Maybe that was why he never tried to purchase the business from Buck and Faye, he decided.

By the time he finished his next to last delivery at the dog kennels, darkness had descended. A steady mix of rain and stinging sleet pelted Bill in the face as he climbed back into the cab of his truck, having collected a check for last month's delivery. Waving goodbye to the owner, Terry Melton, he maneuvered out of the driveway back on to the hard road. Bill wondered how anyone could put up with the din of a hundred dogs barking incessantly all day and night. And how could they stand the smell of all that dog manure, deciding that no amount of debt could make him do that for extra income.

It was an idea his daughter had proposed now that she was living back at home and working only part-time since the divorce; an idea that Bill emphatically nixed. It was one thing to raise cattle or even horses, but to raise dogs to sell…, he couldn't bring himself to do it. Cattle served a purpose, he tried to explain. They produced food that sustained you. And horses, well, horses could be eaten in a pinch he waffled, and besides, they were necessary for working cattle or hunting if you were up in the mountains out where Scott was now living. Dogs were just…, dogs. They didn't graze. They ate food you had to give them every day, not to mention water, and made a mess you had to clean up after. Though he didn't say it out loud to her, he thought it humiliating work.

After twenty minutes and one stop to scrape off the ice accumulating on the windshield despite the defroster going full blast, Bill pulled up the gravel driveway leading to Beth Huffman's place. The burnt-out shell of a house loomed in the headlights as he pulled forward in low gear trying to remember where the propane tank was located. It had been over a year since he'd been out here to move the tank after the fire, after someone had anonymously paid the Huffman's long overdue gas bill. In an effort to help, a group of local volunteers set up a used double-wide trailer directly behind the destroyed house. Bill had offered to go out and move the tank on his day off.

Beth's husband died in the fire which occurred while she was at work on the night shift at a local poultry-processing plant, the second of two jobs she worked, the first being a cashier at the Dollar General store in Willow Brook. Rumors circulating after the fire had Sandy, her husband, making meth in the house since a neighbor up the road, taking in the warm night from a rocking chair on his front porch, described to the sheriff an explosion he heard coming from the direction of the Huffman property. A story backed up by the sweet smell of ether that greeted the local volunteer firefighters when they arrived at the scene, not to mention Sandy's recent history of unemployment and previous run-ins with the law concerning controlled substances and forged prescriptions initially written for their son, Jeff.

The house was engulfed in flames by the time they began pumping water on it, according to one volunteer fireman from Bill's church. He added they found Jeff lying unconscious in the tall grass of the unkempt yard, thirty feet from the house, next to his overturned wheelchair, later finding Sandy's charred remains in the smoldering rubble, next to a bathtub.

Since then, the poultry plant had shut its doors leaving Beth with only a minimum wage paycheck from the store.

Bill knocked on the front door of the trailer, still grimacing from the pain in his back, having slipped on the ice-coated wheelchair ramp that was missing any sign of a handrail. After hearing an incoherent shout from inside, he waited sullenly at the door, catching his breath, while the sleet, sounding like birdshot as it hit the metal siding of the doublewide, morphed into the quiet softness of falling snow. Out of the corner of his eye, he saw a half cord of wood piled haphazardly underneath the partially-skirted trailer, away from the rain and snow, with a maul lying in the bare dirt beside it.

"Who is it?" A soft voice inquired from just inside the door.

"It's Bill Dennison, with Tri-County Propane. I've come to fill your tank," he shouted.

The deadbolt slid, the doorknob turned and there, peering out from the half-opened door, was Beth Huffman, wearing a tattered housecoat, frayed around the collar and cuffs, over slacks and a blouse with dingy pink slippers on her feet.

"Come in, come in," she offered, motioning to Bill with a big wave of her hand. "Golly, it's getting cold out there. My goodness, is it snowing? Oh, it's pretty. I'll have to take Jeff out on the front stoop. He loves the snow."

"Well, be careful," Bill cautioned, "'cause that ramp is slick as snot. I fell walking up it to your door."

"Oh my," Beth consoled him, touching Bill on the coat sleeve with her hand. "Are you okay? I wondered what that thump was a minute ago. It scared Jeff and me. The sleet hitting the roof was driving us crazy. He started yelling. Loud noises upset him. Then the knock at the door came, and well, I just lost it. I forgot you all were coming out tonight."

She paused to catch her breath and, despite the smell of wood smoke permeating the close confines of the trailer, Bill could smell perfume; the same Jenny Martens wore. Ever since his surgery his senses seemed heightened, Bill thought.

Or perhaps he was just more appreciative of those things he rarely acknowledged before his ticker went on the fritz.

"Well, I'm going to go out back and fill your tank. It is around back isn't it? Then, I'll come back in with the receipt to collect."

"Yes, it's over by the utility pole," she answered in a soft voice, pointing in the general direction of north. "I'll go turn on the yard light, but don't you want to warm up first? I can make you a cup of coffee. It'll only take a minute. I'll bet your hungry, too. I didn't know you all worked this late, though I'm awfully glad you do."

She looked at him, her big brown eyes devoid of any sign she'd taken the hint about paying before he left. Biting his lip, Bill decided to come right out and tell her she had to pay tonight, in cash, but she began to speak again.

"I tell you what. I'll have some steaming coffee and something hot to eat whipped up on the stove for you by the time you get done out there."

"No, no, you don't need to bother doing all that," Bill admonished.

"It's no bother at all. Jeff and I haven't eaten yet, either. It'll be nice to have some company for supper."

She opened the door. Bill hesitated but went out, brushing against her housecoat, without asking how she planned to pay.

With the ground saturated, he dared not pull the heavy truck off the drive and risk getting stuck. The wet snow allowed the hose to slide easily across the thick, boot top-high grass to its full length just reaching the rusted round tank. Bill saw the needle touching the peg marked with a zero on the gauge. Thinking it was stuck he tapped it, but it didn't budge.

How is she going to cook anything with no gas, he wondered, thinking he'd have to check the pilot lights on her stove, water heater and furnace, too, if she used them. What a way to live, paycheck-to-paycheck, grocery bill to electric to bill, with no light at the end of the tunnel. Bill shook his head. They'd be better off dead, but they couldn't afford the funeral.

Having filled the tank, placing the lid back over the gauge and coupler, he began the task of rewinding the hose, stopping once to consider the possibility he might have to drag it all back out again to empty the tank, if, god forbid, she didn't have the money to pay.

The heavy hose hung on the corner of an abandoned dog house, halfway back to the truck. Abandoned, Bill decided, since no animal scurried out as he tipped it on its side in an effort to free the hose, though he distinctly remembered a dog from the last time he was out; remembered because of the howls of laughter coming from the boy as he and the dog wrestled in the grass, oblivious to the world around them. Its name escaped him, but he could picture it, a short-haired shepherd-collie cross with a white ring around its brown mid-section and at the tip of its tail.

After knocking at the door to announce his presence, Bill cracked the door to the trailer and hollered to let them know he was coming in.

"Come right on in," he heard Beth Huffman yell from another room, followed by nonverbal but nonetheless human sounds. I'm back here in the kitchen with Jeff. Come on back here and grab you some hot coffee."

Bill hesitated, explaining, "My boots are wet. I'd better stay here by the front door."

"Oh, don't worry about that," she said, sticking her head through the doorway from the kitchen into the hallway, laughing. "As you can see, I'm not much at keeping the house clean. Just take them off if it's a worry to you."

Bill crept across the room in his stocking feet toward the kitchen, taking in the look of the cluttered living room, ducking his head unnecessarily, not used to the claustrophobic closeness of the low ceilings in these old doublewides. Dorothy would be clucking like an old hen if she saw the inside of this place, he mused. She was a stickler for cleanliness and wouldn't think of letting Bill in the house with boots on.

"I hope you don't mind microwaved, turkey hot dogs. It's the only thing I'm good at cooking in a microwave oven. I'm used to cooking on the stove, but I ran out of propane a couple of days ago. It just slipped my mind. I'm so spaced out these days," Beth explained.

"No, I don't mind. I eat 'em all the time at home," Bill offered; a white lie.

He was used to eating homegrown beefsteaks and roasts, detesting anything with turkey in it except during the holidays. Though the cardiologist had chastised him about eating too much red meat after his bypass surgery, Bill had ignored the advice, until now.

He stood next to the Formica-topped dinette set, across from Jeff. Pulled up to the table in his wheelchair, a short string of drool hanging from the corner of his tilted head, he stared blankly back at Bill.

"Jeff, can you say hello to Bill, the propane man?" Jenny asked, saying this as she handed a cup of instant coffee to Bill.

"Mepopain! Mepopain!" Jeff shouted, his head and upper body jerking sideways with each utterance as his arms stayed immobile at his side, as if his hands were tied behind his back and he was trying desperately to free himself from bondage.

Bill looked at Jeff, just for a moment, trying not to stare, but pulled back to the wreck of a young man like any "rubbernecker" at a car crash, before glancing at Beth, standing next to him, for an interpretation.

She laughed, more like a girlish giggle, "He's saying, 'Mr. Propane, Mr. Propane'."

Bill managed a stiff smile and looked back to Jeff, nodding his head in approval, like a first grade teacher acknowledging a completed, though botched, first recital of the alphabet; or a master, urging his young dog to bring the stick *all* the way back.

Jeff had been irrevocably damaged at the promising age of thirteen in a dirt bike accident at a friend's house while the two of them were riding double. As they topped the apex of a hill on the gravel road that fronted the house, a road frequented by a NASCAR-inspired neighbor late for work one sunny summer morning, they met the neighbor head on. His friend was the lucky one, Bill thought: he didn't survive.

That was almost five years ago, as best Bill could recollect about the accident, an accident that sent Sandy, Beth's husband and the father of their only child, into a downward spiral of overdue hospital bills, injuries unable to be coped with, poor judgment and a general cascade of bad luck that culminated in the house fire. How Beth managed to cope with it all herself was hard for Bill to imagine. He sat there watching her feed Jeff some chopped up turkey hot dogs and mashed lima beans that Bill stoically forced down also, helping himself to a glass of water from the kitchen faucet afterwards.

At forty-two, Beth was still a "looker" from Bill's perspective, still possessing the tight, smooth facial skin and pert, firm body of a woman half her age, noticing the housecoat covering her work day outfit had come undone.

"How do you stay so fit and trim?"

Beth laughed, glancing at Bill. "Oh, I don't know, between work and taking care of Jeff, I burn a lot of calories. With Sandy gone and no paycheck from the poultry plant, I've had to pull Jeff out of the special school and take care of him myself. Pushing him around day and night keeps me in shape."

She was staring past Bill and Jeff, strumming absent-mindedly on the collar of her blouse with long slender fingers. Bill tried to think of something to keep the conversation going as he moved his eyes from the coffee cup in front of him to Jeff before settling on Beth again.

"Say, didn't you used to have a dog? I remember your son and him having a great time rolling around in the grass the last time I was out here. What was his name...," Bill paused, trying to think, watching Beth bring her finger to her puckered lips as he continued, "… 'Buddy', wasn't it?" He shouted, glad he'd been able to recall its name.

"Buuee! Buuee!" Jeff began to caterwaul.

Beth hugged him, pushing his face against her soft midsection in a trying effort to quiet her son while explaining the outburst to Bill.

"Bu…," she caught herself and instead silently mouthed the dog's name toward Bill, who was still glancing back and forth between her and her agitated son. Then she slumped into the chair next to her damaged son, putting her elbows on the table before rubbing her face and glistening eyes with the palms of her hands.

Jeff began to calm as she started in again to explain. "He got sick a couple of weeks back. I took him to the vet, but the cost to fix him was just too much," she said, her voice quivering. Shaking her head, she continued, "I just had to have him put to sleep. I couldn't afford to feed him, anyway," she rationalized, biting her lip. "He dearly loved that dog. Damn near drove me crazy asking about him afterwards," she confessed with a forced smile.

Bill swallowed hard, thinking not only of the poor dog and Jeff, but of the invoice in his pocket. Their conversation moved forward in fits and starts as Jeff fidgeted about in his wheelchair until a long silence ensued, signaling its end.

"Well, I guess I better hit the road," he stated, rising from the table. "I sure thank-you for the coffee and food. It hit the spot."

"Now, don't fib to me. Heck, I know you're used to something better than wieners and lima beans," she offered with a short laugh. "There's no need to rush off, though. I don't get many chances to carry on a meaningful conversation with an adult anymore. We're always so busy at work. And Jeff, well…."

By the time she finished, Bill had fished the invoice out of his pocket, placing it on the cluttered table in front of him, unable to lift his eyes from the yellow slip of paper.

"Uh, the total for the gas comes to a hundred thirty-six dollars...., that's with the two percent discount for cash payment," he added after a pause, as if that fact alone would turn her gray skies to blue.

"Oh my, I..., I didn't...," she covered her mouth as she rose from the table, not able to finish the sentence and, unwilling to look at the bearer of bad news. She reached over, taking the ticket before turning quickly to leave the room.

"I'll be right back," she muttered, bumping into the door jamb as she scrutinized the invoice held close to her face.

Bill stood by the table watching Jeff's head bobble as he muttered incoherently and half-heartedly nodded toward the counter. After a moment to decipher his utterance, Bill reached for the on/off switch of a small television on the kitchen counter, and to his relief, this silenced Jeff.

Almost forgetting the pilot lights, Bill called after Beth Huffman, "Where is your furnace and hot water heater? I need to make sure the pilot lights are on before I leave."

"I haven't been using the furnace, just the hot water heater, and I only light it once a day when I have a shower and give Jeff a bath," she shouted from somewhere toward the back of the trailer. "You could light the oven for me. I have trouble getting it lit."

Bill struggled with the oven, finally getting the blue flame to stay on after lying prone on the floor and reaching the gas inlet through several tortuous moves.

Beth returned, daubing a tissue to her cheek with one hand while clutching a small purse with the other.

"I'm sorry, Bill, I mean Mr. Dennison, I thought the price was only going to be seventy dollars. It was only seventy cents a gallon last time."

"Well, sure...," he huffed, out of breath as he sat up on the kitchen floor, "but the price of propane has gone through the roof these last couple of months. I can't let you charge, boss's orders. I'll have to take some of the gas back out of the tank."

He cut her off with this last statement as she was about to speak, knowing all too well what she was going to ask. "Mister Dennison", Bill thought, they all got a lot more formal when they started angling for a reprieve, a payment schedule more to their liking. What they didn't understand or more likely didn't care about was that once Bob Tisdale put a customer on "cash only", he meant it. So much so that it came out of the driver's pocket if a "cash only" customer got gas and failed to pay. It was a hard and fast rule. Bill thought for a moment about Jenny Martens chastising him for having no heart this morning. She should've saved that speech for Bob Tisdale. Jeff began to wail in the background, again.

"Mepopain! Mepopain!"

Bill looked at Jeff, at the television, finally, at Beth, tears streaming down her face, waiting for a translation that didn't come as she slumped down into a chair searching every corner of her purse. Jeff became more animated, pouring out vowels and consonants like alphabet soup.

Beth, laughing weakly, explained. "He always gets worked up when he sees me crying. I'm sorry. I know it bothers you."

Turning her attention to Jeff, she continued in a soothing tone, "It's okay Jeff. I'm fine, just fine. See, I've got a big smile."

Bill sat there on the floor, a solemn expression on his red face, embarrassed, not knowing how to interact with this damaged young man, still like a small child in his actions.

"Maybe, we can work something out," she said, watery eyed, turning back to Bill. "I'm so tired of chopping wood. I'd dearly love to run that furnace just for a day or two."

She stood up, slapping her hands against her side, one still holding the yellow receipt, the other holding a wad of crumpled ones and fives.

"The other guy, Jake…," she stopped, watching Bill grimace as he struggled to get up from the floor.

His back still hurt from the fall on the ice and now his legs were numb from sitting too long on the hard floor. But

Bill was thinking about the wood. He couldn't picture his wife or daughter ever chopping wood. And Jake, what the hell did he have to do with this?

"Here, let me help you up."

Dropping her money on the table, Beth grabbed his arm and pulled while Bill pushed himself up off the cracked linoleum. It was then, while Bill rose up on his feet that he noticed her slender legs peeking out from below the frayed edge of her housecoat. He could have sworn she had slacks on before. Yes, that's right, he thought, she had on her work clothes from the store when she answered the door. Standing erect, he glanced sideways at Beth. Her housecoat was fastened with a cloth belt, and her trembling left hand clutched the top of it closed at the collar. Bill couldn't help wondering if her blouse was gone, too.

"Are you okay?"

Bill took a step, shaking one still-numb leg. "Yep, yep I'm okay. My backs a little stiff from the ice and my legs went to sleep while I was lying on the floor trying to get that darn pilot light going. You're right, that thing is hard to get lit."

Bill limped back and forth between the kitchen and hallway, giving himself time to think, under the guise of getting his legs working again, searching for an answer that would make everything right, something fair for everyone involved. Her mention of Jake stuck in his craw, and Jake's comment this morning flashed through his mind. Bill had to admit he wasn't a great thinker, but he didn't need Bob Tisdale's help to figure out what was going on here.

He stopped pacing long enough to see Jeff and Beth staring at him. One opened mouth with a string of saliva bridging his lips the other tight-lipped with tears, gazing intently at him for guidance.

"Look, Mrs. Huffman…,"

"Call me Beth."

"Look Beth, I think we can work something…," Bill hesitated, rubbing the back of his neck, avoiding both sets of eyes. "Mmmm, can we go in the other room to talk, away from him?" He gestured toward her son.

"Yes, yes. Let's go into the living room first," she offered, taking Bill by the arm, directing him out of the bright fluorescent gleam of the kitchen.

"I'm sorry; it kind of bothers me to talk in front of your son, Jeff."

"It's okay. I understand. You're not the first to tell me that."

Bill's shoulders relaxed as they moved into the dimness of the living room. The only light was a red, throbbing glow, coming from the wood stove in the corner.

"Don't worry about the propane. I'll take care of it," Bill offered, his large hand caressing her on the back between her shoulder blades. He could feel her muscles tense under his touch.

"Dotheep, Dotheep," Jeff howled from the kitchen.

Bill jerked his hand away, as if he'd just touched the electric fence surrounding the lot where he kept his herd bull.

"Why's he saying Dorothy?" Bill asked in a rush.

"Dorothy?" Beth laughed, "No, he's saying, 'Go sleep, go sleep'. He thinks I'm going to bed and forgot him."

Bill felt his heart pounding under the quilted jacket, felt the dampness on his forehead. Was the doctor right? Is my heart as good as new?

"Boy, it's getting cold in here. The wood must be about burnt up," Beth hinted, testing where Bill's heart lie, as she rubbed her folded arms briskly with her hands.

"You know what? Let me go out and split a little of that wood I saw beneath the trailer. I'll bring a big pile in here to keep you going all night and maybe even tomorrow. Meanwhile, between the two of us, we'll figure out what to do about the propane invoice," Bill said.

The cowbell clanked as Bill stepped through the door.

"Well, there he is, Mr.-I'm-never-late-for-work, Bill Dennison," Jenny announced, standing beside her desk, hands akimbo.

Jake and Isaac looked up from the logbook.

"Glad you could make it in this morning, Bill," Jake snorted, staring intently at his wristwatch.

"He's keeping banker's hours," Isaac chimed in.

Jenny giggled.

"I see you guys are hard at it. Trying to figure out how to throw the most work on me today, are ya?" Bill asked, not with the usual gruff tone he used when talking to Jake and Isaac, but instead, a happy-go-lucky voice backed up by a broad smile.

Jake countered, "Dorothy must have got your purple pill prescription filled before you went to bed last night."

"Jake, you're terrible," Jenny chastised, giggling.

Bob Tisdale's office door opened, and out stepped one of Cole Counties finest, hat in hand, badge shining.

"Hey, Bill," Bob Tisdale shouted, waving as he stepped out behind the deputy into the main room. "You were right about the nurse tank. Somebody cut the locks on the gate and the pump during the night and stole over a hundred gallons of propane as near as I can figure."

Bill had a surprised look on his face before his eyes narrowed. "You sure one of these two didn't just forget to lock up after they left?" He motioned toward Jake and Isaac.

"Bill Dennison...," Jake exclaimed as Bob continued.

"No, no they were cut," he said, shaking his head.

Bob Tisdale escorted the officer to the front door, deciding to follow him on to his patrol car.

"With the price of propane and the economy like it is, it was bound to happen sooner or later," Bill offered to no one in particular.

"At least they shut the pump off and closed the valve so the whole tank didn't empty out," Jake replied in a somber tone.

"I wouldn't want to meet the thief. It took a heavy pair of bolt cutters and some strong arms to cut that lock on the gate," Isaac added.

Jake nodded in agreement. Bill began to empty his coat pocket full of receipts and checks onto Jenny Martens desk.

Gritting her teeth, Jenny looked up at Bill from under her reading glasses. "Well, how'd you make out at Beth Huffman's? Did she have any money to pay?"

"Naw, she didn't have enough money to bother dragging out the hose."

"You didn't put any gas in her tank?" Jenny asked, flabbergasted.

Bill snapped, "She was a 'cash only' customer, right?"

Jenny Martens shook her head, biting her lip. "You would of thought after having to pay cash last time..., Jake wasn't it you who filled her tank last time. Why you'd of thought she would know she had to pay. That poor woman she's been to hell and back twice in the past five years. How are she and that boy going to keep warm?"

"Ah, she's got a wood burning stove, right Jake?" Bill said, waving off her concern.

Jake didn't respond.

"Hey, Isaac, are you still interested in buying my bow? I was thinking about it on the road yesterday...."

"I thought the doctor told you to quit doing that," Jake cut in.

Bill ignored the remark, "If you still want it, I'll sell it to you for two hundred dollars."

"Maybe we could take up a collection and pay to have her tank filled," Jenny argued solemnly. "I mean how is she going to cook?"

"She's probably got a microwave. What more does she need?" Bill groused.

"Yeah, let her go to our competitors. They're not as hard-hearted," Jake added.

Jenny clucked her tongue against the roof of her mouth and went back to sorting through yesterday's receipts. The cowbell clanked.

"Say, Bob, you got a minute?" Bill asked, falling into step behind Bob's brisk pace as he headed back toward his office.

"Sure, sure Bill. What's going on?"

Bill lowered his voice as he closed the door behind them. "I need to see about taking some time off for me and my wife's anniversary."

Whitman Whiz Kids

"Now, you're sure you're not gonna electrocute yourself, Billy?" Henry Dean Anderson asked in his shrill voice as Billy composed himself in front of the restless audience.

Henry Dean and Billy stood at one end of the grade school cafeteria behind a table flanked by an American flag hanging limp on a pole at one end and a white flag emblazoned with a green 4-H symbol at the other. We all—in anticipation—leaned one way or the other to get a view around the person sitting in front of us along the three parallel rows of tables that stretched away from their crosswise one.

"Oh, Henry Dean, relax and go sit down, will ya? This is Billy's third year of 4-H electricity projects. Shoot, he's this close to being a master electrician," Randall Stanislauski commanded.

He held his thumb and first finger an inch apart, signaling Billy's expertise. The other hand, after patting Henry Dean jovially on the shoulder, was behind his back—fingers crossed—as he returned to his seat having helped Billy carry his project to the table at the front of the room. Billy Bridwell proceeded nervously, slowly, to give a somnolent explanation of his 4-H project; a treatise on hooking three lights in parallel versus in series.

I'd be lying if I said I wasn't nervous myself when I had to get up in front of the crowd and give a talk. In fact, I don't think there was a future politician amongst us in the Whitman Whiz Kids 4-H Club, named after the rural township most of us called home. Getting up in front of forty people was no one's idea of a picnic; even if, apart from Henry Dean and a few attending parents, most of the audience was between the ages of eight and eighteen.

Billy finished his speech, picked at his pimpled face, and wiped his sweaty palms on his pants before bending down to plug the wires into the electrical outlet to show us what happens.

What happened is this: a blue spark shot out from the other end of the bare wires. This coincided with a loud pop and at the same moment the lights went out in the cafeteria; all a result of the wires having been crossed clandestinely by one of Randall Stanislauski's seven brothers earlier in the evening while Randall had kept Billy preoccupied.

The crossed wires blew a fuse, plunging the room into darkness. The mid-May sun had already set and the rising moon was no help since the window blinds were still closed because of a film we'd been watching earlier called "Proper Record Keeping for Fun and Profit" before Billy's turn up front. I couldn't see my hand in front of my face, let alone the face of Gary Casselbaum, my best friend sitting in the chair next to me.

"Keep your hands off me!" one of the girls in the club shouted through the blackness from the next table over. It sounded like one of Billy's sisters, Vicky Bridwell, and the command was in concert with the distinct sound of a hand slapping bare skin. All of us with mothers knew that sound.

"Now, don't panic. Don't panic," Henry Dean said in a panicky voice. "Billy, are you still alive?"

There was a mumbled response from the front of the room where we last saw Billy. A couple of metal folding chairs crashed to the floor and one of the heavy tables scooted noisily; the result of our 4-H leader stumbling toward the front of the room.

"Has anybody got a light?" Henry Dean asked, hoping someone might have a pen light in their pocket.

Two of the oldest Stanislauski brothers, Matt and Miles, whipped open cigarette lighters and held them aloft. The flickering flames from the stainless steel Zippos revealed a dejected Billy still standing next to the table with his electrical project laid out in front of him. His face wavered in the orange glow of the flames. A faint cloud of acrid-smelling smoke hung in the air above him.

Matt Stanislauski was gingerly rubbing the side of his face. Vicky's hand had hit its mark.

"Well, Billy, you don't look any worse for the wear," Henry Dean offered, looking him over from head to toe, afraid to touch him. "Miles will you go see if you can find Mr. Schmidt. Tell him the lights are out here in the cafeteria."

"I'll go help him," three other boys shouted in unison, myself included, figuring where there was a cigarette lighter, there might be a cigarette. By the time we would find Mr. Schmidt, the ancient janitor, asleep in some dark corner of the boiler room, the shared cigarette would be history.

"No, no, no," Henry Dean admonished in his staccato rhythm, "Miles is capable of finding the janitor by himself. And don't stop to smoke a cigarette, either."

Henry Dean may have been born at night, but it wasn't last night. His voice was high-pitched with excitement, just like when he was judging the hams of an exceptional Chester White hog. An accomplished and sought-after swine judge throughout the state, his excitement, when examining a prize-winning hog as he described it for a ring-side crowd of onlookers, was unparalleled.

Chester Whites were his favorite breed. In fact, he raised them for a living on a small farm he shared with his elderly parents.

"While we're waiting on the lights, does anyone scheduled to give a speech want to volunteer to go next? We've got lots of work to get done tonight."

"In the dark!" Somebody at one of the other tables protested.

"Pretend you're listening to a radio report," Henry Dean chirped.

If enthusiasm was a trait required of a great 4-H leader, Henry Dean wore the crown. But for the rest of us, 4-H club meetings were just a reliable excuse to get out of the house and socialize with our friends.

"I'll go," I half shouted after a quick calculation and no offer from anyone else.

"Are you nuts, Jimmy?" Gary whispered to me in the blackness. "You must be running a fever."

Somebody else made kissing sounds that brought on a low round of snickers from the darkened crowd.

"All right, Jim," Henry Dean said appreciatively, recognizing my voice, "see if you can make your way to the front without stumbling over anyone."

As a rule, nobody volunteered to go first on nights they were scheduled to give a talk or to demonstrate their project. The reason being was that our esteemed leader was forever getting off the subject at hand; the result of multiple obscure questions asked by all those scheduled speech-givers due up next in line.

Before you knew it, he was off on a tangent, our time was up, and the meeting had to be adjourned with half the scheduled speakers given a reprieve until the next meeting two weeks away. This trick only worked during the school year when we had to be out of the cafeteria by nine o'clock.

After the school year ended (which was only a week away) and the weather turned nice, we held our meetings at members' houses, usually out on their lawns, and didn't adjourn until everybody scheduled to speak or demonstrate their project was finished, no matter how late it happened to be.

Now, I wasn't nuts or sick as Gary supposed. And I wasn't an ass kisser as some unseen accuser would have everyone believe. I just figured if I talked real fast I could be done with my speech before the lights came back on. Not being able to see my peers would make talking in front of them a lot more tolerable, I reasoned. None of the Stanislauski clan or Gary and his brothers would be making faces at me, at least not that I could see.

"Are there any questions or comments?" I asked, my speech done in record time.

The lights came on just as I finished my speech though I wasn't quite done scratching my crotch. Smiling sheepishly, I could see half a dozen spitballs scattered about the floor and on the table in front of me.

Henry Dean never failed to comment after every speech; usually a constructive criticism. "You probably ought to slow down a little bit when you talk, Jim."

Hah, my plan had worked, I thought.

Nor did he forget to ask a pertinent question.

"Which will have leaner meat at the same weight, Jim, a steer or a bull?"

My speech had been about feeding cattle for slaughter. I was already inching my way back toward my chair as I responded.

"A bull."

"That's right. Now, stay up there!" Henry Dean whined, like the turbo charger on a diesel engine. "There might be some other questions for you."

Sure enough someone raised their hand. I made a mental note of who it was so I could even the score when their speech time came. It was Blackie, another of the Stanislauskis so named because of a discolored front tooth.

Nervous as I was, I paid no mind to the actual question. Instead, I fell back on my fail-safe answer.

"Don't know for sure, maybe," I said, trying to look thoughtful by scrunching my eyebrows together and jutting out my faintly whiskered and as yet, unshaven chin.

This pat answer worked well in almost every situation outside the classroom with just a few exceptions.

What's your name, son?

"James T. Kelsoe. My friends call me Jim."

How old are you?

"Fifteen. Six more months and I'll be able to drive."

Were you born on this planet?

"Don't know for sure, maybe."

Are you learning anything in school?

"Don't know for sure, maybe."

Do you have any family?

"Don't know for sure, maybe."

"Are you getting any nookie?"

That last question was just asked by Mule, another one of the Stanislauskis.

He'd whispered it to me, cupping his hand over his mouth, trying to break my deep-in-thought-expression as I passed by him.

"If I want any more lip from you, Mule, I'll scrape it off my zipper," I answered sotto voce, out of ear shot of Henry Dean but not my cohorts. My vocabulary expanded exponentially when talking to others if they were close to my own age and not too much bigger than me.

Just a quick explanation of how Jason Stanislauski got the nickname "Mule".

According to his brothers, it was bestowed upon him by his haggard mother when he was just a toddler; something to do with his belligerence at being potty-trained.

Henry Dean was answering the question directed at me as I sat down. I was relaxed and smiling, satisfied that my speech-in-the-dark plan had worked, as well as my quick retort to Mule's question. Then, I fell all the way to the floor as Larry Casselbaum, one of Gary's older brothers, sitting on the other side, pulled the chair out from under me.

The guffaws interrupted Henry Dean as he answered the question in painful detail; something about why you couldn't feed raw soybeans to cattle. I may have known the answer, but, like I said before, "don't know for sure, maybe", was a conditioned response of mine, sort of like Pavlov's dogs. The bell could have been ringing in announcement of a bathe and dip but they would all still be salivating in anticipation. Likewise, my response, no matter the question, was the same.

The meeting lasted another hour through two droning speeches; one on growing vegetables and one on the proper hoof care of a horse. The latter given by Debra Ritchner a seventeen year-old vixen that had everyone's attention.

Well, at least every male in the room that wasn't blind or neutered. One thing I have to say for Henry Dean, he showed no favoritism to the girls in our 4-H club, asking them questions and critiquing their speeches same as the rest of us. Unlike some of my lecherous, male teachers at Westerville High who seemed to fawn over the girls in my classes, especially the good-looking ones that wore extra short skirts.

"Now Debra, what happens to a horse's hooves when it founders?"

Her lilting voice was met by wondrous, slack-jawed stares.

Of course, and I'm no expert here, but Henry Dean didn't have the aura of a "ladies man" anyway. A bachelor, pushing fifty hard with graying, thinning hair and still living at home with his folks, on a hog farm no less; the girls probably didn't have much to fear from him. He had a Pillsbury Doughboy physique that clashed with his pink cheeks. His attire, without fail, consisted of a slag-gray shirt and matching pants, similar to what convicts wear in prison. Put a fake beard and a red suit on him and he would have made a great Santa Clause except for the laugh which would have sounded like it came from one of the younger elves; a eunuch no less.

The meeting ended with the customary refreshments (another reason most of us attended). These consisted of soda pop and cookies or brownies brought by a designated member and hopefully baked by their loving mom. Unless it happened to be one of the girl member's turn, in which case the fare was burnt banana bread or melting peanut butter bars; their early experiments at cooking with the rest of us being used as guinea pigs.

While Gary and I probed the refreshment table for the telltale signs of who'd done the baking, Henry Dean would give us a recap of the agenda for the next couple of meetings. We were getting close to the end of the seasonal 4-H ritual, which was highlighted in late June by a Saturday morning trip around the township to look at everybody's livestock projects.

The members with inanimate projects like woodworking, flower arrangements or, in Billy's case, electrical engineering, brought their projects to the meetings. The rest of us prepared to show ours off on the renowned cross-country road race on the last Saturday of June. I mean you couldn't very well bring in a 250 lb. barrow and set him on the table where Billy Bridwell's project had just gone up in flames. Maybe a yearling heifer or a nanny goat could have been led into the building, but the splatter effect from the inevitable mishap would have been unappreciated by Mr. Schmidt.

"So don't forget," Henry Dean shouted over the boisterous crowd gathered around the refreshment table, "the next meeting is at John Temple's house. Jake Stanislauski is to give a talk on candling eggs and Teresa Fugate will give her talk on breeding gilts."

I nudged Gary Casselbaum in the ribs with a sharp elbow at this last bit of news and watched him turn red-faced with some cola dribbling out the corner of his mouth. I knew he had the "hots" for Teresa.

With kinky auburn hair and an underdeveloped chest, the gangly Teresa Fugate was no Debra Ritchner, but then Gary was no Robert Redford either. One night, when I'd stayed over at his house, he'd confided in me his carnal attraction for Teresa. Said she had a way of showing pigs in the judging ring that made him have wet dreams. I scooted over to the far edge of the bed for the rest of that sleepless night.

The last bit of business before the meeting adjourned for the night had to do with complaints from the previous summer's project tour. It seems there were comments made to Henry Dean concerning the large number and excessive speed of the cars and pickups as we went from one member's house to the next during the season-ending tour. Henry Dean reminded us to find other members to share a ride with so there wouldn't be as many vehicles and the resulting dust cloud from the gravel roads wouldn't blanket the eastern half of Knox County or be visible from the Apollo space capsule orbiting above.

"It's not a road race. And remember," Henry Dean shrilled, "no one is allowed to ride in the back of a pickup truck."

This last edict had been the result of an incident during our tour two summers ago when one of our fellow members fell out on a sharp curve and spent a week in the hospital with two fractured ribs and a broken arm.

I'd planned on riding with Gary and his older brothers though I hadn't asked him yet if it would be okay. I knew there would be room in Barry Casselbaum's old Plymouth Fury, the one Terry, the next oldest Casselbaum, was about to inherit since Barry had just announced his enlistment in the Air Force. A choice we all judged as a wise move. Even though the war in Vietnam was about played out, no one was too keen on joining the Army or Marines just yet.

On the other hand, I'd probably be stuck in the back seat next to that knot-head Larry who had just made my shit list after the stunt with the chair. Maybe, I thought, by the day of the tour I would be able to come up with a way to pay him back with interest. Besides, riding with the Stanislauski clan in their mom and dad's cherry red Oldsmobile Vista Cruiser station wagon was out of the question. In addition to the eight brothers, there were two younger Stanislauski girls in the 4-H club that would have to be carted around, making for cramped quarters in their blue-smoke belching Oldsmobile.

The entire Stanislauski brood, minus Steve, the oldest, and, like Barry Casselbaum, a recent enlistee in the military (in his case the United States Navy), made up fully a quarter of the Whitman Whiz Kids 4-H Club. More than once, when Henry Dean was too harsh with one or another of them for not having a speech or project ready at the prescribed time, they'd threatened to break ranks and form their own club.

This threat always subdued Henry Dean, who was unduly proud of the fact that he was the leader of one of the largest clubs in the state. He hounded us to keep our projects current and in top shape for the best shot at winning during the local fair which entitled you to a slot in the competition at the state fair. The more entries at the state fair, the better the leader of the 4-H club looked. Between his Chester White's and the Whitman Whiz Kids, Henry Dean's life was complete.

I lived on a ten-acre plot of land that my father had purchased seven years ago when he was first transferred here by the company he'd worked for since before I was born. Besides my father, there was my mother and an older sister who was home now only on weekends when she could find a ride back from the college she was attending, a four-hour drive away.

With my parents both working, I had the run of the place for parts of the day between arriving home from school and their return from work. The ten acres included a brick bungalow and a two-story barn that had been part of larger farmstead before being split off and sold separately from the tillable land at an estate sale. My mother had insisted on living in the country when we moved here, wanting fresh country air and a huge vegetable garden, the latter to be supervised by her and slaved in by my now absent sister and me.

Our "ranchette", as the real estate agency had listed it, was split in half by a creek lined with cottonwood and willow trees which ran diagonally across the property. This topography made a livestock enterprise the logical option and since the old barn had only a dirt floor, raising hogs was not a good idea. Thus was born my 4-H project consisting of two Angus heifers and a crossbred steer.

Gary Casselbaum lived on a hog farm four miles west of the "ranchette". With no driver's license yet, no car anyway, and my sister's horse six feet under from a bout of colic last fall, I wore out a ten-speed bicycle going over to Gary's when the weather permitted after school. When his chores were done, and even when they weren't, we played basketball with his older brothers until dark, stopping only when ordered by Barry or his dad to go feed this or that pen of hogs.

Raising hogs seemed so much easier than cattle, at least as a 4-H project. They didn't have to be broken to lead or have their hair brushed everyday like my heifers or the steer that my father had christened "Sir Loin" in anticipation of the day he would grace the new gas grill my father had received as a Christmas gift. All Gary had to do was make sure the round metal feeders, whose loud, clanking lids, flipped open and dropped all day long by the pigs' snouts (a constant reminder it was a hog farm), always had feed in them. Those pigs led the "life of riley".

Heck, as a group, the hogs even shit in the same place making cleaning up after them a piece of cake compared to the mess my three could make all over the barn.

On show day at the fair, Gary would wash 'em off with a garden hose and a little soap. Then, depending on whether they were one of the white breeds (he'd sprinkle those with talcum powder) or dark-skinned Hampshire's (he'd mist a little baby oil on them) and presto; they were clean and shiny, ready for the show ring. No leather show halters to polish no hooves to trim and paint, just aim them toward the show ring and slap them with a leather crop now and then to keep them out of the corners and in front of the judge's discerning eye.

The only down sides I could see to the hog business were two-fold. First was the smell, which permeated your clothes after an hour of working in close quarters with them. And while it washed out of your clothes, the odor clung to your skin no matter what brand of soap you used. It just wore off slowly of its own accord. Even blind-folded, I could tell the hog farmers from the smell of their hands, which, incidentally, made Teresa Fugate a viable candidate for Gary's affections. Their smell cancelled each other out.

The other problem that bothered me was the aggressiveness of the old sows. Gary and I made it a point not to go in the pens with the pregnant sows. Even when one of his older brothers went in a pen with them, they carried a club of some sort. In fact, once I watched from beyond the fence, while Larry got chased around by an irate, expectant Yorkshire momma. Luckily, he was carrying a ball peen hammer. He used it to tap on the side of the metal feeders to loosen the finely ground feed that had a tendency to cake to the walls due to moisture. On that particular day, he beaned the old sow right between the eyes after she'd lunged at him and ripped his blue jeans, drawing a rush of blood from a gash she'd made with her teeth on his lower leg.

Gary and I were both laughing as the sow rolled her eyes and staggered drunkenly backward before collapsing to the ground.

"Dad's going to be pissed when he finds out you killed one of his sows," Gary chastised.

Our twin smiles turned to frowns as we realized Larry still had the hammer in his hand and was scissor jumping over the fence, heading in our direction, madder than a hornet.

"Save yourself!" I shouted at Gary as we took off at a dead run, splitting off in different directions to puzzle "Short-fused" Larry.

Larry was no dummy though. He knew I was the slow-footed one from playing basketball with us and had me down on the ground before I'd made it to the end of a long row of brown wooden farrowing crates. The only mercy he showed me after stuffing ground-up corn cobs (they'd been spread on the dirt lane to fill in the mud holes) down the back of my pants was to flip the hammer over in his hand and start whacking me over the head with the wooden handle. By now, Gary had come to my rescue and jumped on Larry's back.

"Goddam it, Gary, if you're gonna ride me, buy a saddle!" Larry yelled.

"I don't need anything to ride a weanling filly like you."

That remark got me laughing all over again. Larry was about to blow another gasket until Terry Casselbaum cooled him down by turning the water hose on us as he washed off the nearby concrete slab of a finishing pen. After a few more cross words from Larry while he fingered the new hole in his pant leg, we all gave up and went about the task of removing the dead sow from her crate, pooling our intellectual resources to come up with a plausible explanation to present to their dad on why he had a 400 lb. dead sow. Larry had inherited his fiery temper from his dad, who would be upset, to say the least, at the site of a deceased source of income.

Still, we couldn't pass up the chance for some cheap entertainment at the expense of the dead. After propping the stiffening sow against a sycamore tree, her butt on the ground and her four legs sticking out in front, I loaned her my ratty baseball cap and Gary retrieved a pair of sunglasses off the dash of their old farm truck to rest on her snout. Barry wedged one of their dad's half smoked cigars in her mouth while Terry and Larry, using a broken-handled pitchfork and some baling wire for strings, balanced a make-shift guitar atop her outstretched front hooves. The collective hope was that a little humor might defuse the situation.

That day, I made it a point to head for home as soon as I heard the senior Casselbaum's tractor coming in from the field, leaving my hat and the Casselbaum brothers to explain the sow's untimely death; not sure of their dad's sense of humor. Twice on the way home I stopped to shake the crumbled corncobs out of my pant legs as they migrated towards my high tops.

On the last Saturday in June, we were to rendezvous at the Oak Grove Christian Church parking lot. It was centrally located and the plan was to make an irregular shaped circle around the township to visit every 4-H member's farm before ending up at Henry Dean's place where he would sign off on all our record books. They had to be completed in order to enter your project at the local fair.

When asked by Gary, Barry Casselbaum, in an unusual display of benevolence, agreed to come by and pick me up on their way to the church. Most times he cut me no slack and I would have had to bike over to their house despite the fact it wasn't out of their way to pass our "ranchette" on the way to the church.

Gary said when I called to beg a ride that Barry's date with Uncle Sam had been pushed back three weeks. According to Gary's psychoanalysis, Barry was being extra nice to everyone lower on the food chain in hopes that the powers that be would somehow get the message to his drill sergeant and he would return the favor. Fool, Gary and I thought, though we were smart enough not to share our wisdom with Barry.

When Barry wheeled the Plymouth Fury, complete with chrome, rooftop, luggage rack, into the gravel parking lot across the road from the church, three cars were already there. Our esteemed leader hadn't arrived yet nor had the Stanislauskis. As soon as Barry cut the engine, a distant rumble rolled across the church parking lot. It came from the east through the century-old oak and maple trees that ringed the clapboard church and its surrounding cemetery whose tombstones shared the same last names as many of our 4-H members.

Gary and I rushed to exit the backseat of the Fury after another of Larry Casselbaum's remarkable bouts of on-demand flatulence. Staring down the chip and sealed road (one of only three in the township), we saw the telltale signs of the Stanilauski's overtaxed Oldsmobile approaching. A thin cloud of blue-black smoke clung to the top of the first of a series of four hills that marked the approach of the road to the church from the east.

Just then, in a flash of red, we saw them top the second hill and could hear the big V8 engine building rpm's as it gathered speed with the help of the earth's pull on the descent. The sound decreased to a deep, dull hum just before the engine screamed complaints as it tried to break its grip on gravity on the ascent toward take off speed and the peak of the second hill.

Squatting on the parking lot adjacent to the road, I kept my eyes on the crown of the hill as I picked up a hand full of pea gravel, a surprise present for Larry Casselbaum's shirt when the time came. Gary and I could see a flash of daylight under the front tires of the Olds Vista Cruiser station wagon as the front grill came parallel with the earth heading due west before plunging out of sight on its way back down to the valley of the final hill. We could also hear the faint screams of the two Stanislauski girls as the sound wave swept past us.

"You know, Gary," I announced, springing to my feet, "I believe I'm going to go stand on the other side of your car just for an added bit of protection."

Gary thought the situation over before deciding to join me.

We stood on the leeward side of the car, joined by the rest of the Casselbaum's, poised to make a dash for safety if circumstances dictated.

Just then the red beast topped the last hill before the church. This time there was no doubt it could fly. All four tires released their contact with Mother Earth, and the gleaming Vista Cruiser broke free of gravity, if only for a second. Miles spun the steering wheel as the front end re-entered the atmosphere putting the car into a sliding stop across the parking lot. When she came to a stop, the wheel still cranked all the way to one side, he floored it and did donuts, showering us with pea gravel, stopping only when the tires began to smoke.

With Larry Casselbaum distracted by the flying debris, I took the opportunity to dump a hand full of sand and gravel down his tucked in shirt.

Two more cars and a pickup truck pulled in as we caught up on the latest gossip with the Stanislauskis. Mule complained about his sisters' screams as he shook off the effects of sitting between them. With the help of his brothers, me and the Casselbaums, we resurfaced the parking lot with our shoes as best we could before Henry Dean arrived.

Victor and Teresa Fugate pulled up next and I caught a glimpse of Gary as he reached inside his pants pockets to adjust his underwear. I pointed out this breech of etiquette.

"Sorry, Jimmy, but I've got 'Injun' shorts. They keep sneaking up on me."

"Spare me the details, Gary," I begged.

Next, John Temple came down the road doing a wheelie on his recently-purchased 250cc Yamaha. Desperate for a car but with not enough money for even a "rice-burner", I broached the subject of going halves on a motorbike.

"You know Gary, I've been thinking." Ignoring the roll of his eyes and a terse comment, I continued. "Since neither one of us has enough money for a vehicle maybe we could pool our resources and buy a motorcycle like John's there. We could keep it at my house in the barn and take turns using it."

"In your dreams, buddy," Gary snorted.

"Why not? Hell will freeze over before either of us have enough money for a car."

"Two reasons Jimmy boy: number one, if my calculations are correct, and they most certainly are, I'll have my driver's license in three weeks and two days whereas you, my friend, have four long months to go so we couldn't possibly keep it at your house; secondly, and you've already touched on the subject, what are we going to do in the winter time when it gets cold as hell around here? Are you going to ride it to school when its fifteen degrees outside? Besides, with Barry leaving in three weeks; only Terry and Larry stand between me and the old green Plymouth here."

He tapped proudly on the rusted, dented hood like it was a Corvette or something before continuing.

"A slip off the top of the ol' grain bin for Terry, a fall into the pond for Larry, and who knows; I might be driving this car before school starts."

"Geez Gary, I had no idea brotherly love ran so deep in your family," eyeing Gary's diabolical look as I spoke, deciding he was even more desperate for a car than I was.

Gary turned his attention back to Teresa Fugate and I proceeded to try a different tack.

"I don't know, Gary. I mean summers already a third over. Why waste the rest of it. If we..., I mean, if *you* had a motorcycle couldn't you just see yourself flying down the road with Teresa over there, her arms wrapped around your belly..., or maybe even lower; her kinky..., her soft, wavy hair touching your thick, muscled neck as she leans forward and whispers in your ear or better yet as she nibbles on your earlobe before licking you with her tongue; her cotton sun dress blowing up around her waist while you squeeze her bare, naked thigh with one strong hand; the other one twisting the throttle grip all the way open, a rooster tail of dust pluming skyward behind the two of you as you head west into the setting sun."

"How much did you pay for that bike, John?" Gary inquired, licking his lips.

The price was too much, Mule Stanislauski insisted, standing there beside us now, eavesdropping. Like, how the heck would he know, I thought, trying to do the math in my head. *Could I come up with half that price?*

I watched out of the corner of my eye as Teresa Fugate tugged at the hem of her paisley dress, pulling it down past her bony knees within an inch of the top of her rubber boots; no doubt a result of Gary's glaze-eyed ogling.

Just then two more cars pulled in and finally, Henry Dean's powder blue Chevy pickup turned the corner, the stock racks swaying in rhythm with the undulating road.

"Well, how are all the Whitman Whiz Kids?" Henry Dean squealed, "What a glorious day for our project tour, don't you think?"

There was a collective groan and nodding of heads in response.

"It looks like we're still short a few people. Who's that over in the cemetery..., by the oak tree?" Henry Dean asked, squinting his eyes and shading them with one hand on his forehead. "Is that Larry Casselbaum? Is..., is he going to the toilet on those sacred graves?"

His voice reached a glass-shattering crescendo at "sacred graves".

"He's waving at us with one hand so he's just taking a leak," Mule Stanislauski surmised.

"No..., no, I think he wants some toilet paper," I offered, not yet ready to forgive Larry for the 'corncob incident'.

"Larry Casselbaum, get your butt over here!" Henry Dean shouted at the top of his lungs right next to my ear drum.

I was beginning to sympathize with Mule's complaints about his sisters' screams on the thrill ride over here.

Larry finished putting his boots back on (I'd managed to pour a full load of gravel down his shirt) and sauntered back towards the parking lot. Henry Dean, red-faced with indignation, was going a mile a minute, shaking his head, pointing at Larry emphatically.

"What a disgrace. I can't believe it. Larry Casselbaum taking a..., was he really taking a dump in the cemetery, in broad daylight?" he asked, looking at me only because I was still standing next to him, the ringing in my ear just beginning to subside.

I shrugged, "Don't know for sure, maybe."

Larry, oblivious to Henry Dean's fury and walking more comfortably with the gravel out of his undershorts and boots, gave a big howdy as he approached. With that slack-jawed I'm-innocent-but-really-guilty look on his face, it took Larry Casselbaum a full two minutes of unwavering denial (all the while with the Stanislauski brothers wrinkling their noses and sniffing the breeze) before he convinced Henry Dean he was innocent of a bowel movement on sacred ground. This was followed by a teeth-chattering blow to the side my head from "Short-fused" Larry when Henry Dean's eyes were averted.

Two more vehicles coasted to a stop beside us and we were ready to begin the annual 4-H project tour-de-Whitman Township.

"We're going by Debbie Richtner's place first since she only lives a couple of miles from here and she told me last night on the phone she has to leave for cheerleading camp in an hour," Henry Dean explained.

"What about her record books?" someone asked over a background of smooching sounds.

"She can bring them over to my house for approval when she gets back," Henry Dean answered.

"She can bring them to my house for approval anytime," Barry Casselbaum whispered, already back behind the wheel of his car.

Hmmm, I thought, perhaps I've miss judged Mr. Henry Dean Anderson—lady's man extraordinaire.

"Now remember, there isn't a prize for being the first one to each stop, so take it easy with the driving," Henry Dean admonished, climbing back into the cab of his truck.

Miles Stanislauski was already throwing gravel before Henry Dean's door had closed. But only for a moment, as he had to stop while Blackie let down the rear door of the station wagon and pulled one of his forgotten sisters, running full throttle, into the car.

"No one will catch the red beast-mobile," Miles shouted from his window.

But it was too late. Barry cut in front when they stopped to let the wayward sister in. John Temple was trying to cut across the recently mowed hayfield adjacent to the church parking lot on his bike. Too bad he'd forgotten about the new five wire fence on the other side of it next to the road ditch, and, unless he was planning to pull a Steve McQueen ala The Great Escape, he was screwed.

Our Plymouth was in the lead as we turned the corner on-to a gravel road and the rest of the caravan vanished in our dusty wake. An old Credence tune blasted from the eight-track player mounted under the dash.

"You think Dad would let Jim and me buy a motorcycle?" Gary shouted out to no one in particular.

Terry Casselbaum turned around in the front passenger seat and Larry leaned forward to see around Gary. Both were looking directly at me.

"Is this another one of your bright ideas, Jimbo?" Terry queried.

"Yeah, like the corn kernels at the Tri-County Fair last summer?" Larry added.

"Hey, now hold on a minute, that was highway robbery. We were cheated. I mean, despite the outcome, you've got to admit it was a brilliant idea," I countered.

"Brilliant my ass," Terry huffed, waving me off with his hand.

I couldn't believe they were still sore at me over that episode eleven months ago.

Memory-like-an-elephant Larry chimed in, "That reminds me. You still owe Terry and me for the sack of corn and five-gallon bottle of water we bought for your scheme."

Now even Gary, seated next to me, had a disgruntled look on his face as he remembered the bleak details. My motorcycle dream was fading faster than the Stanislauski's Oldsmobile.

The incident that the sour-faced Casselbaum brothers were referencing started innocently enough at the Tri-County Fair held every August, a week ahead of the State Fair.

Gary and I, bored with watching the pigs sleep, decided to peruse the business displays set up in a row next to the carnival midway. Central National Bank had a big tent set up with all kinds of freebies: paper pads, ink pens and yardsticks, with their logo of course, laid out on a table along the front.

At the end of the table was a large glass water bottle, the kind you see in an office, like a bank, with a chintzy paper cup holder on the wall next to it. This glass bottle, which had a volume of five gallons, was full of shelled corn. The sign beside it explained that whoever came the closest to guessing how many kernels of corn were in the bottle would win a five hundred dollar cash prize.

Well, right away I figured how to tip the odds of winning entirely in our favor and break the bank so to speak.

"Genius, pure genius," Gary whooped, slapping me on the back when I explained to him my plan, causing me to lose the three blocks of fresh bubblegum I'd just placed in my mouth.

The bubblegum came courtesy of the Knox County Republican Party tent. Between them and the Central National Bank, our pockets were stuffed.

Upon our return to the hog barn, Gary and I convinced Terry and Larry of the merits of my scheme. Enough so that they agreed, in exchange for a split of the prize money, to purchase a sack of shelled corn from the local feed store and a bottle of water which they had to search all over town to find.

I don't know if they appreciated the fine quality of that bottled water or not, but we dumped it on the Casselbaum's show hogs to cool them off and filled their water trough with it anyway. Gary's and my part of the deal was to fill the empty water bottle with the corn, then dump it out and count the kernels.

This financial arrangement with Gary's brothers was necessitated by the loss of our own money the night before while trying to win a prize at a carnival air rifle game. Gary kept telling me the game was rigged. And I kept pouring money into the game, his money too after mine ran out. But how could I doubt the sincerity of a raven-haired woman, wrinkles an inch deep across her face, a missing front tooth with a spent cigarette dangling from the corner of her lips and wearing a halter-top. She was the genuine article; a bonafide carnival barker.

"You're just about to win it, handsome," she confided to me after each near miss. Looking back, I think the vapors of her cheap perfume clouded my judgment.

We counted that damn corn three times, only because "I'm-gonna-be-rich" Larry kept interrupting me to make sure I was doing it right, causing me to lose count. The three counts were off but not by much. I figured in my razor-sharp way that we would just enter several times to make up for any discrepancies in the averages.

Back at the bank tent, Gary and I, with serious looks on our faces, filled out the entry forms and placed them in the box next to the bottle. Some swanky, sweaty, good ol' boy wearing a blue tie and a pink, once-pressed shirt, showing the effects of the mid-summer heat, came up from behind the table and spoke to us.

"Hee, hee, you young fellas think you know how much corn is in there?" He chuckled and smiled, an unctuous smile, and pointed at the bottle.

"Don't know for sure, maybe," I offered with a shrug.

Gary chimed in, "Oh, we know exactly how much is in there. We cou..."

I tripped, almost knocking "Big Mouth" Gary to the ground before he could finish.

"Hey, come on Gary. It's time to feed the pigs," I said tugging on the back of his shirt, towing him out of the tent before chastising him. "Nice going, Gary. You just about spilled the beans."

"Sorry, Jimmy. I was thinking about how I was going to spend my share of the prize money," he replied.

And that's exactly what I did for the rest of the week the fair was in progress. There wasn't any way we could lose.

I checked the mailbox every day for the next week, waiting for the envelope confirming me or Gary as the winner. It didn't come. Then, in the next day's paper they listed the winner. Some schmuck from a town I'd never heard of. The whole fair was rigged, I thought.

I found a state map in the glove compartment of my mom's car. Sure enough there was a town by that name eighty miles west of here. Geez, don't they have their own fairs over there?

I promptly called Gary to tell him the bad news. He said he'd just got done reading it himself. In an unusual lapse of ethics, I told him it might be best to discreetly tear out that part of the paper and feed it to the hogs so his brothers wouldn't see it.

Now, eleven months later that lapse came back to haunt me.

"Come on little brother," Terry said sweetly, menacingly, from the front seat, rubbing his thumb and first finger together in that universal language, "It's time you and Dumbo, I mean Jimbo, paid up."

"Yeah, pay up or we'll have Barry stop the car and tie you both to the luggage rack," Loan Shark Larry added. "Ten dollars ought to cover principle and interest don't you think, Terry."

Terry nodded in agreement.

Well, luckily for Gary and me, Barry wasn't about to stop the car and let the Stanislauskis catch up, which was a good thing since there wasn't ten dollars between me, Gary and the cushions of the car seat.

About that time, the eight-track player started to malfunction, or so I thought from the loud rumble I was hearing. Just then I turned to look out the rear window. Through the chalk-colored dust I could make out the front grill of the red behemoth only inches from the Plymouth's back bumper. Through breaks in the roiling fog dust I could see the maniacal grins on the three Stanislauski's in the front seat, all of them lunging forward in unison as if to give the car a little more forward momentum.

"It's the Stanislauskis. They're right behind us," I shouted.

Barry stomped on it but the Plymouth didn't have much left in her. There was one more curve just ahead before the last quarter mile stretch of straight-away to the Ritchner farmstead. This gave us a little breathing room as the Oldsmobile wasn't very responsive on the turns.

Just as the Stanislauskis were about to catch us again, the Ritchner's driveway came into view. At first I thought Barry must have been daydreaming about Debra or perhaps the next three years in the military or maybe both, because he drove right by the turn-in before slamming on the brakes. We braced for impact. Thank God the breeze was perpendicular to us now, and the view of those behind us was no longer obscured.

"We're going to be the last ones parked," Gary moaned.

"Shut up, you dimwit," Barry commanded, turning to look out the back window, one hand on the steering wheel the other grabbing the back of Terry's headrest.

After the last vehicle—Henry Dean's pickup—hobbled into the driveway, Barry goosed the Fury back around the corner, facing out to the open road, ready to be the pace car again when we took off toward the next stop on the tour.

Right then and there I knew I would sleep well that night and every night that followed. Knowing that with sharp guys like Barry Casselbaum at the helm of our military, we were safe from Communism and whatever else the "Russkies" could throw at us.

The horse was a sway-backed, old nag, but Debra Ritchner looked quite fetching in her blue and gold cheerleading outfit. Her mom even brought out cookies. I know if I was a 4-H leader that would have been ample reason for an A plus on sweet Debra's project.

The next uneventful stop was at John Temple's place to observe his flock of Shropshire sheep. I wasn't much of a sheep man, but like Gary pointed out, they had paid for John's motorcycle, which was more than I could say for my two heifers and "Sir Loin", who were saddling me with an ever mounting feed bill.

On our way to the next stop, Victor and Teresa Fugate's Landrace hog farm, we were hanging back to avoid the dust from the caravan (Miles Stanislauski, a quick study, was the first to leave John Temple's place), and I began to needle Gary about his unrequited love for Teresa Fugate. This was news to the rest of the Casselbaum's, and I was accused by Gary of being a stoolie.

"Do that trick again, Jim. The one where you open your mouth and your face disappears," Gary sneered.

"Teresa Fugate's half crazy," Larry advised.

"She is not," Gary replied in her defense.

Larry argued, "Sure she is. Ask Terry; he saw her talking to the wall once last year at a 4-H meeting."

Larry leaned forward tapping Terry on the shoulder.

"Hey, Ter, Gary here has the 'hots' for Teresa Fugate. I told him she's crazy but he doesn't believe me. You tell him."

"Is she the cute twiggy with kinky hair and pointy tits?" Barry, our doyen asked, not taking his eyes off the road.

Gary protested, "Her hair's not kinky, it's wavy."

"Last year during one of our winter meetings at the grade school, I was headed for the john and when I came around the corner of the hallway outside the cafeteria there she was, talking to the painted, cinder-block wall pretty as you please; not another soul in sight."

Terry was shouting this revelation back at us over the blaring eight-track while looking straight ahead, helping Barry scan the dust cloud for car bumpers.

"You mean she was talking to a blank wall? There wasn't any picture or anything there?" Gary asked, a little shaken by this revelation.

"What the hell difference does that make, dumb ass?" Terry scoffed, glancing back at Gary with a look that asked, are we really related? "Like maybe she was less crazy if she was talking to a picture of George Washington or the Declaration of Independence as opposed to a painted wall."

"What color was the wall painted," I inquired, egging them on.

Larry put in his two cents worth, "According to her mother, she's been a little off ever since her aunt got ate by some pigs. At least that's what I heard her tell Mom one night at a church potluck a couple of years ago."

I looked at Larry, then Gary. I pulled myself up between the seats and caught a glimpse of Terry's face; none of them were smiling.

"Whoa, whoa, whoa. What…, what do you mean she got ate by some pigs?" I stammered, in a high-pitched voice, beginning to sound like Henry Dean, my bottom jaw almost touching the seat. "I've never heard of that! Are you bullshittin' me?"

"No," Terry said, matter-of-factly, "You didn't read about it in the paper? This lady, Teresa's aunt, I reckon her great aunt 'cause I think she was in her sixties, was carrying a couple of five gallon buckets of ground corn across the pig pen towards the feed trough and she tripped near as anyone could figure. Evidently, when she fell, she spilled the corn all over her. The sows, there was twelve of 'em, were extra hungry since they hadn't been fed for almost a day. And next thing you know they were eating her as well as the corn."

"They ate all of her!" I shouted disbelieving. Reason, big, big reason number three for not raising hogs. "Geez Louise, that's disgusting. Was there anything left?"

Terry shook his head, "Nothing but her rubber boots."

"So what's that got to do with Teresa being crazy?" Gary asked defiantly.

"Man, I don't know about crazy, but it's sure making me queasy," I complained, feeling light-headed

"I guess she'd just been there the day before. She was real close to them since her grandparents had been long dead," Terry explained.

"Did they get eaten, too?"

"No, you nimrod, I don't know what happen to them. They probably died of old age or silo gas or something."

"Holy cow! I hope they shot all of them sows," I said trying to stay calm.

"I think her dad and the uncle took them to the sale barn the next day."

"Oh, great," I bellowed, "How many people did they devour there?"

Terry ignored me. Barry skidded the car to a stop in front of the Fugate's paint-deprived, ramshackle house. As the dust settled, I could see Victor and Teresa heading toward an eight-acre pig lot, west of the house and surrounded by a single strand of electric fence wire. The rest of our entourage followed suit, gingerly stepping over the knee-high fence. The familiar, rhythmic, snap-snap sound of electricity arcing between wire fence and metal fence post was a cautionary statement we all understood.

"Hey, Billy," Mule Stanislauski inquired, "How's come all these flies on the fence aren't being electrocuted.

"How the hell should I know?" Billy growled, still sore over having his project sabotaged.

"Well, you're the electricity whiz around here," Mule laughed.

Everyone close enough to hear, had a smile on their face, except me. Taking Mule's question too seriously, my face held a look of puzzlement as I studied the myriad of flies lined up on the strand of wire, parts of it blackened by their feces.

"Mule," I proposed, "Why don't you jump up in the air and grab the fence. Let us know if it shocks the piss out of you."

"That sounds like a capital idea," he responded, more wizened about the ways of electricity than me.

And without hesitation, he put his arm on my shoulder to brace himself as he half-leaped half pushed himself up into the air as he grabbed the wire with his other hand.

Stunned and cursing wildly from the shock, I checked my jeans for a wet spot before giving chase as Mule ran laughing across the barren lot. Faster than me, I settled for what looked like a dirt clot and heaved it at him.

"We're not here to play games, you two," Henry Dean chastised in soprano.

Victor and Teresa had both picked up well-worn, wooden clubs lying next to a dead elm tree just inside the fence as they headed for a cluster of low-slung, tin sheds, half the height of an outhouse but longer and wider, situated in the middle of the lot.

I stayed back in the pack, mindful of the story I'd just heard, keeping the Stanislauski sisters in front of me, thinking, because of their small size, they might appear more appetizing and be slower afoot than myself.

This lot was what I pictured the moon's surface must look like. It was covered in a dusty, slate-gray soil and pockmarked by craters ranging in size from a bathtub to as big as a backyard swimming pool. Two lonely, limp jimson weeds were the only living plants growing across this eight-acre pig sty.

Despite the lack of rain for over a week, the craters were filled within inches of their top with a liquid mix of water, dirt and God knows what else, the consistency and color of potato soup. To call it mud would have been an insult: to mud. In some of the less-frequented craters, a green layer of algae was creeping across the surface like flakes of parsley.

Lolling about in one pool were two momma sows, which Teresa Fugate coaxed out with a couple of rocks, splattering my jeans with crater content as I stood on the opposite side ready to make a break for it if they showed the slightest cannibalistic tendencies. Then, Teresa proceeded to the next crater just outside the rickety shacks where the herd boar was having a relaxing snooze.

"Chase him out of that wallowing hole, Teresa," Henry Dean shouted, wanting to examine the prized stud boar standing on solid ground.

The flop eared 'ol boy took up almost the entire length of his personal cesspool. At one end, his corkscrewed tail stuck up out of the brew like a twisted periscope. At the other, his long snout was resting peacefully on the bank, the surface of that soup touching his jowls just below his beady eyes. The tips of his down turned ears just grazed the surface and gave an occasional flick when an errant fly buzzed too close, causing a ripple to spread across the liquid.

Teresa, with her stick, gave him a love tap on his exposed broad shoulders covered with bristly hair. When he ignored her by turning his head slightly to eye whom was pestering him, with no other inclination to move from his repose, she whacked him between his ears. This got his attention, and with a protesting grunt he stood up, stretched, had his morning constitutional, then proceeded to shake vigorously like a dog come in out of the rain, showering lovely Teresa as she tried to move out of range.

"What a set of hams!" Henry Dean shrilled.

Simultaneously, her brother was squatting and walking into the hog shed looking like a Ukrainian folk dancer. Banging on the inside wall with his club and shouting in pigalese, he roused three more sows who made a concerted lunge for the opening that Victor was blocking.

Unable to move fast in his compromised position, the sows knocked him back out the opening and into Teresa's fleeing path. Teresa, weighing at most a hundred pounds, lost her balance and fell sideways into the two foot-deep crater the herd boar had just vacated, catching herself when only half-submerged.

Victor, apologizing profusely, helped her back out.

There Teresa stood, stunned, looking like someone had just picked her up from a horizontal position and delicately dipped her halfway in the stew, like a ripe strawberry half-dipped in spoiled cream. The rest of the Whitman Whiz Kids and our esteemed leader stood there frozen, silent, waiting for what might happen next.

Turns out Teresa could cuss like a sailor. Still gripping her club, she blew matted, moist, gray-tinted hair from the corner of her mouth then wiped away the goop from the right half of her face with her clean left forearm. Next, letting off steam, she flung the stick wildly with the force of Goliath accidentally whopping Gary upside the head.

"Knight-in-Shining-Armor" Gary was moving toward his beloved to assist in her moment of need when the blow felled him. Undeterred, he got back up and with Victor's help managed to guide the raging Teresa to a garden hose just outside the hot wire fence for a cold shower.

Compared to that, the rest of our project tour was uneventful: Just one minor fender bender, unnoticeable by the parental owners of either the Plymouth Fury or Oldsmobile Vista Cruiser power wagon; and, a bit of road rash experienced by John Temple when his cycle skidded out from under him while taking a short cut across a waterway in the Casselbaum's cornfield.

At the end of summer, my dad got promoted and transferred to an office on the opposite side of the state. I sold my two heifers to a neighbor and got compensated generously by my parents for "Sir Loin"; enough so that later in the fall, after settling in at my new school and turning sixteen, I bought a used car.

After the first, choking, sentimental bites of my filet, expertly cooked on my father's fancy grill, "Sir Loin" went easily down my gullet.

From that summer on though, pork chops have always tasted a little gamey.

The Hat

Denver was our place to meet this year. It was centrally located for all six regional sales managers from the company. With the meetings over for the day, I had reserved tee times at an exclusive club in the foothills west of the city. The low humidity and high altitude, plus a couple of pitchers of beer, had everyone in a talkative mood around the table in the clubhouse.

The topics ranged from cold calls to commissions, from embarrassing moments to times of elation after a big sell, before focusing on politics. With the Presidential election only a month away, it was on everyone's mind. In turn, Martin Sorenson, middle-aged and at the top of the pack sales-wise—and a thorn in my side—wanted to tell us a story that, he supposed, seemed somehow appropriate to the topic at hand as well as the times we were living in.

Martin, even before I was promoted and became his boss, always kissed up to me, almost as if he were mocking me and my ethnicity in a manner I couldn't defend against. I'd been pushed to the point of carrying a tape recorder in hopes of him blundering in such a way that I could terminate him, with justification, to my own boss, a bone-headed "whitey".

"Yesterday, I was reminded of a hat, a discarded, urine-soaked hat that almost got me killed," he said, stopping to wipe away perspiration from his high forehead with a hand-kerchief.

His ribald stories, always good for a laugh or cry, had everyone's attention. The setting sun was balanced on a mountain peak beyond the window behind him, like a circus seal with a beach ball balanced on its nose. Martin, leaning back in his chair, hands clasped and resting on his healthy paunch was within its corona. None of us could peer directly into his face as he continued.

"As you all know, for twenty-five years now, since graduating from college, I've lived in a white, middle-class neighborhood in a Midwestern city of a half-million people, and I make no apologies for it," he summarized, glancing in my direction.

Our young, Latino waiter interrupted him, setting another pitcher on the table. Martin, waving off everyone else's attempt to pay, handed the waiter a soggy twenty-dollar bill, explaining to him in broken Spanish that he could keep the change. Then he resumed his story.

"Yesterday, during the middle of the day, during the middle of the week, the doorbell rang while I was packing. Upon opening the door, standing in front of me was a black kid, an unusual occurrence in my part of town. I say kid, but hell, at my age now, everyone younger than twenty looks like a kid."

Others around the table, a halo of tobacco smoke beginning to rise above them, grunted their understanding.

Martin began again. "He had his sales-pitch down pat, something about selling magazine subscriptions to earn points toward a scholarship for college. He wore a new-looking baseball cap sideways on his head, just like in the music videos. It had a Yankees insignia on it, much to my chagrin, but his accent didn't match the hat so I cut him some slack. Also, he had several—I assumed fake since real ones would have been counterproductive—gold chains with medallions hanging from his neck. 'Bling', I believe is the term they use nowadays for those accessories.

"Isn't that right, Tyrrell," Martin asked, looking at me.

I nodded, a sour look on my face.

"But it was the hat more than anything that caught my attention, and it left me speechless for a moment while I recalled a memory from my college days. Out of character, I decided to buy a subscription from him. Hell, truth be told, I bought two and watched as he skipped up the street to the next drive where he disappeared from view. Still, I stood there reminiscing about that damn hat."

Martin stopped long enough to take a long draw from his glass and refill it. His thick, scarred fingers were evidence that he hadn't always been a salesman.

"It wasn't a fancy hat, like a homburg or a fedora; this was the eighties. Those kinds of hats had been out of vogue for more than a generation, seen now only on the heads of our fathers and grandfathers at church on Sunday mornings or at the occasional funeral service. No, this was a cap, a well-worn baseball cap to be exact. And it wasn't like these polyester and plastic mesh ones everyone wears today, handed out free by companies with their name on 'em. This one I'm talking about was made out of wool or felt or whatever baseball caps used to be made out of before their manufacture was outsourced to Bangladesh.

"I don't remember the logo on it, though I'm sure it was neither of the two teams we went to watch that night at old Comiskey Park. You see the hat wasn't mine. It belonged to a friend of mine, Dave Jewel, whom I'd known since before high school. The hat, stretched and tattered, dated back to those days, so I suppose it had some sentimental value to him since he always wore it, although I suspect that was in part because he was going prematurely bald, like his old man."

There was a slight commotion as several around the table rubbed a hand self-consciously through their thinning hair.

"Dave and I, along with two others, Jesse and Bill, had taken the Amtrak train bound for Chicago to meet up with Steve, one of Bill's old college roommates and, our poker buddy. At the time, I was the only one of us in possession of a car. But it was less reliable than the train schedule and in constant need of expensive repairs.

"Steve had graduated from college the previous semester and lived back at home with his aunt and uncle in a near-west suburb by O'Hare Airport. He worked an entry-level position for an insurance firm down in the Loop just off LaSalle

Street. During college he had worked along with Dave and Bill, at the Deluxe Bar and Grill, a respectable establishment near campus.

"Myself? I worked part-time, three nights a week for a private security firm that did government contract work. Sounds impressive, eh? In reality, I was an ill-trained, baggy-uniformed security guard at an Army Corp of Engineers research lab situated in an industrial park out by the interstate on the edge of town.

"It was an easy job, and, if you discounted the irate callers threatening to blow up misconceived flood-control dams, poorly designed river levees, or the lab itself, a safe job. Religious extremist, Islamic Jihad, and terrorist cells weren't a part of our vocabulary yet. The Black Panthers, Weather Underground and S.L.A. were melting into an expanding, tolerant society.

"My boss, an easy-going sort, who ran a private detective agency in addition to the fledgling security company, said that as long as I made the hourly rounds of the complex—three brick buildings adjacent to a cornfield and surrounded by a ten-foot high, chain link fence—I could do whatever I wanted for the rest of the hour. If I trotted, I could pare the entire circuit down to less than twelve minutes.

"My intentions were to study for the remainder of each hour until my shift ended at two o'clock in the morning. Getting paid while I studied—I thought I'd died and gone to heaven.

"Turns out, the place wasn't conducive to studying. I spent most of the time between rounds daydreaming, sleeping, or going toe-to-toe (I was a philosophy major at the time) over the phone with the crank callers.

"As for Jesse, I never knew him to have a job. He got by on whatever obscure scholarships, grants, and student welfare he could finagle from the gullible financial aid department at the university. In addition, the periodic sale of various bodily fluids for research and fertilization, at the affiliated medical school, supplemented his income.

"Now, back to the hat. The four of us made our way up out of the cavernous spaces of Union Station into the brilliance of modern humanity. Everyone shielded their eyes from the mid-day August sun—except for Dave, because of his hat. The Windy City streets were teeming with lunchbound hordes of office workers; men and women of all ages dressed to the "nines", a far cry from the lax dress codes of the college crowd we were used too.

"We caught the 'El' for a ride west toward Circle Medical Campus and the studio apartment that Dave had recently rented. He planned to transfer to the Chicago branch of the university this fall in hopes of matriculating into their Pharmacy School. It was a curriculum suited to him since he was already well versed in most recreational drugs with an emphasis in the hallucinagenics. Our plan was to drop our gear at Dave's new apartment before heading over to Steve's home to start our weekend revelry, heading back to crash at the apartment afterwards.

"Dave's apartment was new only in the rhetorical sense that Dave had never lived there before. In reality, it was the antithesis of new. The apartment was up three rickety flights of stairs none of which lie in a horizontal plane using the street as a reference point.

"It consisted of two rooms plus a tiny bathroom just big enough to comb your hair in. The kitchenette's linoleum floor was covered with a plethora of faded stains in multiple colors highlighted by several black burn marks. The living room-bedroom combination had a cracked window that faced the alley. A rug, worn through in places to the coarse-weaved, brown backing, covered the floor. The plaster walls had half a dozen amateurishly repaired holes each of which approximated the size of a fist. Dave said the place was a steal at the price he'd paid. It looked to me like the only thing that could be stolen in this neighborhood was as person's wallet.

"Dave had lived in low-ball places since high school. We all had. It was a simple fact since money was always the over-riding issue in any decisions we made during that time of our lives. My creed in college had become, 'if you can't say something nice, don't say anything at all'. Since I couldn't always keep my mouth shut and feared biting my tongue, I tried something nice.

"'Well, Dave, you won't have far to go in order to outrun the locals on your way to campus at night. And it's nice that you got a room with a view,' I offered."

"Jesse snorted, 'Shit Dave, you've lived in some dumps buddy, but this place takes the cake.' Jesse had a different creed and ignored any thoughts of etiquette. 'And the view I'm getting from your window is of some old codger taking a piss in the alley.

"Everyone gathered around the window to see if Jesse was jerking our chain, but sure enough, below us, only facing the building on the opposite side of the alley, was a bum hosing down the brick wall in broad daylight. It looked like he was trying to spell his name. Either that or he was already too drunk to stand still in one place.

"Dave, while pounding on the window, shouted, 'Damn it, I'm not putting up with that crap around here.' As if his presence in the neighborhood would somehow uplift it.

"'Open the window so I can toss something at him,' he barked, already heading toward the kitchen in search of any throwable object.

"Three layers of paint and a settling foundation made opening the window a challenge, but a rust-pitted razor blade and a couple of abandoned kitchen utensils belonging to the previous tenant did the trick. By then, though, the public micturitionist was already hobbling on up the alley, zipper in hand. Dave tossed a warped butter knife at him as best he could by sitting on the window ledge and leaning out. The knife skittered off the brick pavement and clipped the old fellow on the leg, eliciting only a scowling, half-turned face as he kept moving, albeit at a faster pace.

"'Wow, I think you scared him,' Bill joked.

"'Hey, at least I hit him. That wasn't a half-bad toss from the angle I had,' Dave boasted, satisfied he'd done his civic duty.

"Everyone piled their book packs in the corner next to a broken-down sofa covered in a tweed fabric the color of grass. We traveled light during our college years; whatever you could carry in your book pack sufficed. A change of clothes, toothbrush and paste, a used bar of soap, and a partial roll of toilet paper pilfered from one of the campus-building bathrooms were the necessities; and rarely, if there was room or an upcoming exam, a textbook. Jesse ridiculed Bill for having a full bottle of shampoo and some cologne in his possession; called him upper crust, an elitist, among other things.

"Arguments ensued over the sleeping arrangements, which were: who got the couch, who got the newer-looking velour recliner—it was a furnished apartment after all—and which two got to sleep on the floor with the roaches, a given in any building this old. The only other furniture was a round, three-legged kitchen table and a crippled nightstand with a lamp that had at best a forty-watt, flyspecked light bulb with no lampshade.

"On close inspection, the fabric of the ragged couch had glittery-looking filaments interspersed throughout the green cloth—like tinsel. The consensus among was that, closer to the holidays, Dave could stand the sofa on end, wrap some twinkling, colored lights around it, and substitute it for a Christmas tree; a real money saver.

"We took turns using the head before we left, except for Jesse who was blithely pissing out the open window, laughing like a mad man. The only one of us with a beard, he looked like pictures of Karl Marx I'd seen in books, only less serious.

"'Hey, Dave, this is how you stop them from desecrating your alley. Just piss on them,' Jesse hollered.

"Bill, a native Chicagoan, bellowed, 'Jesus, Jesse, were you born in a freakin' pig sty? This is the city of big shoulders and civilized gangsters. It ain't a public toilet. You "downstaters" are a bunch of hillbillies.

"Though he could be rough when needed, Bill was a bit more refined in the ways of big city manners than us 'downstaters', a term he used as a condescending put down.

"By now, Dave was out of the bathroom and not a minute too soon, or I might have had to join Jesse at the window. Dave was livid and laughing at the same time.

"'Put that thing back in your pants right now, you exhibitionist, or I swear I'll slam the window on it and nail the damn thing shut,' Dave shouted.

"I think he was right though, about the exhibitionist part. In our hometown, Jesse had a history of mooning sidewalk strollers from moving vehicles, streaking down Main Street clothes in hand when that fad was all the rage, and exposing himself at a girl's high school athletic assembly once when he was a junior. All this for laughs, which there were plenty of, but also a few serious detentions resulted. College had been liberating for him; a chance to get away from small town mores. On the flip side, antics that got everyone's attention there hardly raised an eyebrow in a forward-thinking university town. Jesse was forced to up his game to stay ahead of the pack, to be cutting edge, so to speak. His charades and jokes became more grandiose though no less predictable to those of us who knew him."

Being the national sales manager, I interrupted Martin long enough to hand everyone their quarterly performance bonuses and cigars before urging Martin to continue, checking to ensure the recorder in my pocket was still on.

"We arrived at Steve's place ten minutes before he was due home from work. His aunt and uncle let us wait inside out of the heat and humidity of a Midwest summer afternoon; a small leap of faith since they hadn't met any of us before, and none of us were dressed as Bible salesmen. The uncomfortable silence as we sat there was like waiting downstairs at a first-date's—the only daughter of a Baptist minister— house while being scrutinized by the minister himself.

"When Steve arrived, the mood lightened. He was like the older brother that showed up in time to vouch for our good intentions; the toll bridge that connected us to the other side. And the toll this time was a twelve pack of Old Style in a condensation-stained brown paper bag he carried under his arm like a football.

"'Stevie, my man, how the hell are you?' Bill greeted him with outstretched arms aiming for a can of beer.

"'Hey, man, it's great to see you guys,' Steve replied, pushing his wire-rimmed glasses farther up his longish nose before sweeping his dark blonde hair off his forehead, all in one familiar move. "I wondered how long it would be until you all missed me.'

"Bill was quick to answer, 'Yeah, well, you know how it is. They don't serve Old Style downstate.'

"Steve smiled, 'You losers, now I remember why I don't miss sharing a house with you guys or working in that stale-smelling flop house, Deluxe; talk about a misnomer.'

"Steve proceeded to shake our hands, something he'd learned since college or, perhaps more likely, a throw back to his pre-college manners, stirred up in him by the reproachful eyes of the couple who'd raised him.

"Steve had done his share of partying with us, but still, he was the quietest one of our group. He was the one with the steady girlfriend until almost the end of his college term, the one who never made a stupid bet at our midnight poker games, the quintessential business major with gung-ho plans instilled in him by his elders with the intention being to emulate them or perhaps escape their shadow.

"'We were all tapped out after the last poker game,' Dave explained, tipping back his cap. 'After thumbing through our Rolodex list of easy marks with money in their pocket, your name came up.'

"'Hah, very funny. I'm not playing cards with you dead beats. I'll bet you don't have enough money between the four of you to ante up for one hand of Three-Card Guts. Where's all your stuff anyway?'

"'We stopped by Dave's luxury apartment before heading over here on the "El". We're going to crash there tonight,' Bill explained.

"Steve gave a puzzled glance in Dave's direction. 'You rented an apartment, here, in Chicago?'

"I could see the wheels turning in his head: someone with an apartment, perhaps in need of a roommate, a chance to get back out on his own. I'm sure it was killing him, living here, after four years of freedom.

"'It's a shit hole,' Jesse remarked. Steve's aunt and uncle frowned.

"Dave, ignoring Jesse's comment, explained, 'You bet I did. It's over by Circle Campus. I'm signed up for classes there when the fall semester starts in three weeks.'

"'Wow, that's cool, man. We'll have to move our poker games to Chicago. There won't be anyone left working for that gay-boy manager, at Deluxe. Well, no one but his bed buddy, Billy Boy, here, and his mustachioed roommate, Mr. Cheswick. Now there's a sick picture; a real ménage`a trois.'

"While saying this, Steve was putting his arm around Bill who was a half a foot shorter but twice as broad. Bill had wrestled in high school, but a back injury had kept him off the mat in college. Steve, tall and thin, was a soccer aficionado, having played on a traveling club throughout college.

"'Screw you, Stevie,' Bill said, ducking out from under Steve's arm. 'You're the one who was kissing his ass back in the spring so he would give you a good reference for your new job.'

"'That's horseshit, and you know it,' Steve shot back.

"'Yeah, yeah, yeah,' Bill responded, rolling his eyes.

"'Uh, not to change the subject but, what kind of fun do you have lined up for us tonight,' I asked, getting antsy to be on the road.

"'Fast women and loose slots,' Jesse wished for out loud.

"'Nah,' Steve said, shaking his head and frowning after a swig of cold beer. 'I thought we could play Pinochle in the den for a while and then go out for ice cream.'

"'Oh, that sounds like fun,' his aunt said cheerily, clasping her hands, before realizing her mistake.

"That stopped the conversation dead in its tracks as we stared at Steve's serious-looking face.

"Then he laughed. 'You morons, I could sell you the Sears Tower. Sorry, Aunt Rita, I didn't mean you. What a bunch of rubes. And you…,' Steve, now speaking sotto voce away from his aunt, was stabbing at Jesse with one finger, the others wrapped around his sweating can of Old Style, 'I couldn't get you a slow bitch, the four legged kind, let alone a fast woman, with you looking like that.'

"Steve was referring to Jesse's bohemian look, with his ripped Che Guevara t-shirt and a pair of holey jeans that exposed both of his pale, bony knees.

"Steve's aunt lowered her eyes to her still-clasped hands resting in her lap, as if recognizing she shouldn't be privy to this part of the conversation, yet unwilling to leave for fear of missing some insight into the life of the only child she'd ever raised.

"'I'm not sure I even want to be seen with you guys. If you haven't noticed yet, I'm moving up in the world,' Steve joked as he brushed his lapel with his free hand.

"He was referring to the sport coat, pressed white shirt and black dress slacks he wore; not to mention the striped tie peeking out of his coat pocket like a rattlesnake, all standard issue in the business world.

"Jesse chided, 'Yeah, yeah, excuse us Mr. Insurance Man or should I say Mr. White-Rat-In-A-Cubicle Man.'

"'Hey, don't knock it. It's a job. And I've almost got enough money saved up to buy a nice car, eh Marty '

"Steve made that last remark to remind me of the time we took a road trip in my car that left us stranded in the Quad Cities for two days when the clutch went out.

"Just then the doorbell rang.

"'Which reminds me,' Steve said, heading for the door, 'I got us a set of wheels and maybe six tickets to a White Sox game if Donnie came through for me.'

"'Okay, everyone, this is Donnie Bigalini. He has a real car.' Steve emphasized as he ushered the newest guest over the threshold. 'Donnie, you may already know some of these losers.'

"Donnie Bigalini, like Steve, had just graduated from the university with a business degree. They'd had several classes together in school, and stayed in touch since moving back to Chicago after graduation. Always on the lookout for potential job upgrades, it's what they call networking nowadays. Donnie had just purchased a used car, a maroon Buick, from his old man who was moving up to a Coupe Deville.

"Steve proceeded to introduce us all in a professional manner. Glancing at Jesse, I could tell what he was thinking from the scowl on his face: three months removed from college and Steve was already turning into a responsible, middle-class adult.

"'I've seen most of you guys at Deluxe or the pool hall,' Donnie said, nodding an acknowledgement to each of us. 'Bill, aren't you one of the bartenders at Deluxe?'

"'Bartender Numero Uno and Assistant Manager on Friday and Saturday nights,' Bill corrected while Steve made kissing sounds beside him.

"'Go screw yourself, you freakin' hermaphrodite,' Bill shot back.

"Ignoring him, Steve continued, 'So, Donnie, did you get a hold of the tickets.

"'You bet I did. It cost me an extra Saturday of work but what the heck. I can't believe you guys are all White Sox fans.'

"We're not," I said too quickly, without thinking. Donnie's reasoning was sound though. South of I-80, White Sox fans were rarer than gay, black republicans.

"'Just ignore that ingrate,' Steve cut in, waving off my comment with the flick of his hand. 'What is important is that you and I are Sox fans. I mean Bill here is a freakin' Cubs fan so we know what a foolish world of futility he inhabits.'

"Donnie nodded his head in sympathy.

"Bill retaliated, 'Hey, I don't recall the White Sox setting the baseball world on fire in the past half century.'

"'Well, it's a moot point anyway since the Cubs are out of town this weekend,' Dave cut in, eager to hit the road. Thirty minutes in a three bedroom, split-level ranch was more than he could bear as a reminder of how his pre-college days had been, before his parent's divorce.

"'I hear ya, man. Let's go,' Jesse chimed in.

"'Let me change clothes, and we'll be on our way,' Steve called out over his back, already bounding down the carpeted hallway to his room.

"A polite thank-you to Steve's aunt and uncle for their hospitality was one of the few threads of civility we still possessed. But a sense of relief was palpable amongst us at being released from this informal inspection by an older generation that had become foreign to us except during excruciating holiday reunions.

"No one really cared that only two of us six in the car were Sox fans. And I don't even remember who they played that night. It just felt good to be out on the town that summer evening with people you were familiar with, despite their irritations. No tests to study for, no bills to pay, no girlfriend to hover over, no thoughts but those that came freely to you in the moment as we drifted south on the Dan Ryan Expressway, windows cracked due to the abundance of smoke. Our conversation went in scattershot directions concerning old friends and new jobs. Maybe, it has to do with safety in numbers; six prime-of-life pals going to a ballgame, like an updated Norman Rockwell painting of the American Pastime.

You know, it's different when you're in a big city by yourself. There's always little part of your brain that won't let you relax; won't allow you to let your guard down—unless you're drunk—no matter how invincible you perceive yourself to be. And our driver, Donnie, a true Chicagoan, not a suburbanite, two generations removed from Italy, seemed sensible enough. He even offered to drink only a beer or two during the game, sort of a designated driver, so the rest of us could party down. What a great guy. What could be better than that? How could anything go wrong? But it did.

"Our seats were good enough; out in right field, one section in from the foul pole and three rows up from the wall; the part of the ballpark where, on a hot August night, the ushers expect a little rowdiness from the fans to make up for any distance from the action and/or dullness of the game. We didn't have a pretty, young usherette wearing short shorts and a low cut top like you get in some ballparks. No, what we got was an uptight, middle-aged man sporting a crew cut and a beer gut, with functional suspenders and a thin, blue cotton vest that signaled his position as an employee of the place. He had that typical, Polish-immigrant look that was ubiquitous to parts of Chicago. He could have been anyone of our fathers, except of course, Donnie's.

"But the worst he did was telling us to tone it down a bit in the later innings. No one had a beef with him, other than Jesse, who, true to form, razzed him at every opportunity. Why hassle him I thought? But then Jesse thought on a different level.

"Someone came up with the not so sober idea that we should drink one beer per inning with the exception of Donnie, our wheel man. We drew matches to see who would buy the first round. The idea being that, with five of us, one lucky sucker would have to buy only one round, assuming the game didn't go into extra innings, and, we kept up the one beer per inning pace.

"Dave, by chance, drew the shortest matchstick and Jesse the longest, meaning that Dave would buy first, and, short of a rainout, would be buying two rounds; but hey, so would Bill and Steve and me, too. This turn of events irritated Dave more than it should have. After all, Donnie held the matches and had no vested interest in the outcome.

"Several side bets throughout the game to increase the excitement didn't go Dave's way either; among them: would Carlton Fisk hit a home run in his next at bat, would the opposing pitcher walk a batter with the bases loaded, would the third base coach tug at his crotch once or twice before spitting. When you're strapped for cash though, which, after paying rent and tuition, I'm sure Dave was, the last thing you want is a run of bad luck. Believe me, I know. The shelves of the library are lined with books that delve into the psychology behind a gambler's bad habits, such as the age-old deception of making bolder and bolder bets—fueled by alcohol-released inhibitions—to make up for earlier losses.

"And to make matters worse, during the whole game, after each lost bet, Jesse kept goading Dave about his 'shithole apartment'; his words, not mine. Just like a toothache that won't go away, that was Jesse's modus operandi. Find a scab and pick at it 'til it bleeds, so long as it was someone else's scab.

"But I knew Dave too well. I knew when it was time to lighten up on him. Jesse knew him too, but it didn't matter to him. He was on a roll. You could see Dave's mood grow darker with each lost bet as the game wore on, like an angry summer sky just before it releases a torrent of bone-soaking rain.

"Nine cups of beer later, the game ended. We sat there for a few minutes, Dave with his cap pulled down low over his eyes, brooding. The rest of us mulled over how to spend the remainder of the evening before our bladders got the best of us, and we headed for the men's room on the way out.

After seventy-some odd years, Comiskey Park was a relic, the oldest major league ballpark still in use and nowhere was this more evident than in the bathrooms, which were antiquated to be polite and decrepit to be blunt. They were built way before individual urinals, or stalls for that matter, became the norm; back when ventilation was an afterthought.

"The community urinal—a long, enamel-coated trough twenty feet in length, eighteen inches wide and sloped ever so slightly toward one end with a drain—was mounted against the cinder block wall. Above the urinal, the paint was darkened by the greasy handprints of countless pissers who had come before to do their duty. The room, reeking of alcohol, cigarette smoke, and an eye-watering level of ammonia, was packed with die-hard fans that'd stayed until the end of the game.

Bill and Steve got lucky. Each found a spot right away and was back out into the fresh air with Donnie while Dave, Jesse, and I waited our turn. Dave garnered a spot nearest the drain where the river of urine ran deepest. Jesse followed with a spot separated from Dave by one scrawny old timer wearing a White Sox jersey. A place opened up for me near the end opposite the drain, up river so to speak. As I approached the trough, I glanced along the row. Everyone had their feet planted, legs slightly apart, one hand on the wall in front of them or both hands below their waist, depending on their preference, staring aimlessly at the blank wall as if in search of enlightenment. They were minding their own business; except for Jesse. He was reaching stealthily behind the shriveled guy to his right as he tipped Dave's cap forward off his head.

"Dave, lost in the stupor of alcohol and the coma-inducing sense of relief from a long awaited urination, was slow to respond. The baseball cap slid down his nose, bounced off his upturning, stubbled chin, and landed square in the deepest part of the swirling eddies of pale yellow urine as it pooled around the drain. That cap soaked up liquid like a thirsty sponge, with only an inch of its bill above the ever-deepening lake of urine as it slowly plugged the drain.

"I swear, for just an instant, time stood still. A dozen men in various stages of sobriety, after registering in their dulled minds what had happened, laughed, laughed boisterously—myself included. But then, as if on cue from a choral director, the laughing stopped, except for the soloist, Jesse, whose laugh now echoed alone off the crumbling walls of the chamber.

"The director we'd taken our cue from was Dave's face. In that instant of misfortune, the effects of alcohol had disappeared from it, replaced, just briefly at first, by a look of bewilderment, then disgust as we laughed. Finally, a look of pure hatred appeared that silenced all of us with a conscience—for lack of a better word. During just that second of silence, a look of guilt—for laughing; then sympathy, for his being vexed by a cruel joke—possessed us all; except for Jesse, whose laughing and hand clapping could be heard as he exited out the door.

"As I look back at that incident, I'm reminded of all the wannabe comedians on cable television these days who, I suppose due to lack of comedic talent, have to rely on the humiliation of others to get their laughs. Sure we laughed then and we still laugh today, almost a simian reflex, a knee-jerk response that can't be stopped. But the humane ones among us try to stifle it as we realize how just as easily we could become the next victim. Jesse was two decades ahead of his time.

"Dave, to his credit, had the foresight to grab the tip of the cap's dry bill before it went under for good and pull the sodden baseball cap out of the community urinal so it could drain again. He flung the hat, dripping, onto the cement floor where it landed with a resounding splat.

"I watched him leave the bathroom as I hurried to finish, hoping to stop a fight that was brewing. Dave's jaw was set and his face was fire-engine red. From fifteen feet away, I could see the corded arteries pulsing up the side of his neck and, if humanly possible, smoke would have been coming out his ears. He was madder than a scrotum-shocked bull at the stockyards, determined to kill the first unlucky bastard that crossed his path.

"When I caught up with Dave and the others out in the corridor, he and Jesse were in each other's face with Dave screaming obscenities and Jesse making faces at him while babbling incoherently like a lowland gorilla. The others wanted to know what had happened, especially Bill, who was trying to get between the two of them in an effort to keep Dave's tirade from turning into a fistfight. Meanwhile, our rowdy gang had caught the attention of two of Chicago's finest, decked out in their checkerboard-rimmed police hats. "'Take it outside!' One of them bellowed in our direction, while his hand made a move toward a glimmering nightstick hanging from his belt as a not so subtle hint.

"Donnie, the most sensible one of us, stepped into their line of sight and, facing the rest of our group, whispered while pointing with his thumb, 'Cool it you a-holes, or we're all going to be in trouble.'

"'What the hell happened in there, anyway?' Bill asked, while we moved as group out into the parking lot across from the stadium, still trying to keep Dave and Jesse apart.

"I gave a brief synopsis, forgetting my college creed. 'Jesse, that fucking dipshit, knocked Dave's cap right into the urinal. What a fucking asshole thing to do.' I was staring evil-eyed at Jesse while I spoke. The response was the same from Bill, Steve, and Donnie as it was from the onlookers in the men's room: a quick snicker followed by a look of disgust as they glanced at Jesse, shaking their heads.

"'Oh, screw you,' Jesse chortled with his usual nonchalant manner. 'It was a joke. It ain't my fault he couldn't catch it in time.'

"Jesse was laughing and slapping his leg. A fake laugh, meant to dig in deep.

"'You asshole,' I said. "How could he catch it in time with one hand on the wall and the other holding his pecker? You knew what was going to happen the second you did it,' I scolded, like a foul-mouthed school marm, as if it mattered.

"Now, I was getting mad. Dave got in the front seat of the Buick, slamming the door shut, at last silent, but still fuming. Bill and I were in the back with Jesse who kept up his harangue at Dave, and now me.

"'You two are a couple of pussies that can't hold your liquor. And baldy up there,' Jesse chided, tapping on Dave's bare head, 'can't hold on to his hat, either. And he's got a shitty apartment to boot.' Jesse laughed once more with a snort.

"Dave flipped him the bird but did a heroic effort of keeping his mouth shut. I was not so controlled.

"'Fuck you, piss ant,' I hissed. My measured replies were a thing of the past now.

"By now we were out of the parking lot, rolling slowly through the postgame traffic. Jesse grabbed Dave's still-waving middle finger, and Dave turned to hit him. Seated next to Jesse, I broke it up before any punches landed, but now, Jesse was slapping at me like a four year-old being harassed by an older sibling.

"I couldn't take it. My fuse was short anyway, and the alcohol shortened it even more. I popped him twice on the mouth, the second one harder, maneuvering in the cramped confines of the mid-sized Buick to cock my arm fully before letting fly again. Jesse, graced at birth with the speed of a garden slug, grabbed at me in an effort to stop the blows, ripping my shirt in the melee as I swung at him a fourth time. I had to swing around Bill who, after being caught off guard, now pushed his way between the two of us while Steve tried to restrain me from the front seat.

"'God damn it!' Donnie shouted over his shoulder, still driving, 'Don't tear up my car, you freaks.'

"Everyone was shouting at one another, except me. I had turned cold and calculating, a hunter in sight of his prey, trying to find a position where I could pummel that bastard, Jesse. At least he wasn't laughing any more, I thought, as the three of us wrestled in the back seat.

"'You Neanderthals, I'm pulling the car over right now,' Donnie was screaming and turning toward us with every other word, watching the road in between. 'If you guys want to fight, then I'll stop the car, and you can get out and fight.'

"'Stop the car,' I said, catching my breath. 'Right now!'

"Donnie obliged me and pulled over to the curb. I got out and held the door open. Jesse was turned the other way, looking out the window on the opposite side. That insidious laugh of his had reappeared, but I knew his mouth and nose were bleeding.

"'Get out of the car you shithole,' I demanded through clenched teeth.

"'Come on, get out of the car,' Donnie hollered. 'I don't want you in my car if you're going to fight. Damn it, are you bleeding on the upholstery?'

"'Get out of the car, you chicken shit, smart ass!' I shouted once more.

"There was silence for several seconds as I stood there bending down to look in the car but could see nothing, blinded by rage. Steve or Donnie or Bill or maybe all three told me to get back in the car; told me to forget about it, that Jesse wasn't going to fight. I still stood there, quivering. I wanted to beat him so bad I couldn't help myself. Wanted to beat him for what he'd just done plus for every other transgression he'd ever pulled. Wanted to beat him as a token of my ingratitude for every stunt, every smart ass in the world had ever pulled on me or Dave or anyone else, for that matter. Finally, Donnie spoke up.

"'Come on, man, get back in the car, or I swear, I'll leave you here.'

"I wiped the sweat from my upper lip with my forearm and glanced around me, seeing only the glare of a few headlights as the traffic thinned now that we were several blocks removed from the ballpark. I stuck my head back in the car and spoke.

"'You're a small timer, Jesse. Your jokes, your stale antics; they stink like fresh dog shit.'

"'Yeah, and I suppose your shit don't stink. Go shoot yourself and put the rest of us out of our misery, you righteous bastard,' he boasted defiantly.

"He wasn't looking at me, but I could see his reflection in the window against the darkness; could see the smirk on his face; could see the dark splotches of clotted blood in his beard. Always a comeback, I thought; the consummate smart ass. I started back into the car, trying to grab him around the neck and drag him out, but Bill and Steve blocked my path.

"'Okay, that's it. I'm leaving,' Donnie warned. He let the car roll a couple of feet then stopped.

"With a heavy sigh, Dave broke his silence. 'Come on, Marty, get back in the car,' he pleaded. 'Everything's cool, man.'

"I stared at him, disbelieving what I'd heard. 'How the hell can you put up with that crap from him,' I shouted. 'You should be out here helping me beat his ass!'

"Dave shrugged his shoulders and turned away.

"'Fuck this shit,' I murmured, feeling betrayed. 'I'm not riding in the same car with him.'

"With that I slammed the door shut and walked across the street, oblivious to traffic or where I was at.

"I didn't blame Donnie for leaving me there. He'd warned me. And Dave told me later they came back around looking for me after realizing what part of town they'd left me in. Yeah, right, like that makes all the difference. Besides, he was worried about his car, plus, before tonight, he didn't know us, only Steve. He didn't know Jesse; hadn't had to listen to his mouth all these years.

"It was Dave, though, who kept me steaming now. How could he blow off the humiliation just like that? Parental guidance? I doubt it. Maturity? Maybe. In the end he was the smart one, a quick study when it came to compromise, I suppose. I had to learn my lessons the hard way, slowly, over the intervening years, but they began the second that Buick pulled away from the curb.

"After cooling off enough to look at my surroundings, I could see I was standing in front of a three-story building that looked familiar. Turns out it was only the architecture that I recognized. There was a defaced map of the campus mounted on an outside wall by the entrance that told me exactly where I was; a nondescript classroom building on the campus of the Illinois Institute of Technology; a deserted island in a sea of destitution.

"I'd never had a reason to venture into this part of Chicago, but I knew of its reputation from the crime pages of the

Sunday Sun-Times and the Tribune. Stepping into the shadows of some bushes near the front door, my mind raced as I considered my options. Like I said earlier, bravado tends to take a back seat to self-preservation when you're alone in the big city.

"This was a foreign country. To be exact, a third-world country, with a language I wasn't fluent in.

Further from the building's entrance, out by the graffiti-covered sidewalk, was a phone booth. Not really a booth, but a newer version—a pedestal with a cracked fiberglass canopy covering the phone—only there wasn't a phone. It had been decapitated, leaving just an array of color-coded wires poking out from where the phone should have been.

"I was cursing under my breath at my predicament when I spied a police cruiser driving down what turned out to be South State Street. Without thinking, I jumped out into the street to flag them down. They didn't see me or chose to ignore me. Or maybe it just wasn't safe to stop. But one figure, walking briskly up the sidewalk, did see me as I slinked back into the shadows of a spruce tree closer to the building.

"'Man, whatcha doin' out here this time a night?' he asked in a rapid-fire manner, shifting a couple of notebooks from under his arm. His voice had the higher pitch of surprise to it, and he looked past me as if searching for the rabbit hole I'd crawled out of.

"'I'm trying to call a cab but the phone is gone,' I mumbled, pointing at the pedestal.

"He shook his head, chastising me. 'They ain't no cab gonna come round here, 'specially after dark. How'd yous get here anyways? Man, a honky like yous won't last long in this part of town. Heck, I'm liable to get in trouble for just being seen with the likes a yous.'

"He stopped to catch his breath. Since I didn't have anywhere to go and not much left to lose, I proceeded to explain to him how I got here, leaving out a few of the bitter details. Though, while I talked, I kept asking myself: How did I get here? It wasn't my cap soaked with urine. I hadn't been the one who'd knocked it off Dave's head into the urinal. I'd been just a sympathetic witness to the whole prank at first. It was a matter of principle I'd stuck up for. The same reason I was too stubborn to get back in that car. But none of that mattered now.

"He glanced at me, and then he looked up State Street for a long while before speaking. His voice had the tone of an older brother explaining to an adolescent sibling about the ways of the world.

"'It's like this man. I'm walking north, all the way past Roosevelt Road. Your best chance is to walk right along beside me with your head held low. Don't take your eyes off the road in front of those boots of yours. If you make eye contact with the wrong "brother", there's liable to be hell to pay. Once we get closer to downtown, yous'll be able to get a cab or bus.'

"'Are you sure? I don't want to get you in trouble. Couldn't I just catch a bus down here?' I offered with the last bit of chivalry I had.

"He laughed, then explained. 'No man, they don't run this late down here in the projects. And if theys did, and yous got on…? Yous wouldn't get off downtown,' he emphasized, shaking his head.

"I nodded, understanding, hoping he hadn't changed his mind about being my guardian angel.

"'Stay beside me, and let me do all the talkin'. If anyone asks yous directly, just say yous with me.'

"And so we started walking, leaving behind the comparative safety of the tree shadows for the well-lit but deserted four lanes of State Street. The undamaged—due to their unassailable heights—sodium-vapor streetlights cast a jaundiced pall over the horizon ahead of us; the last time I raised my head skyward for the remainder of our time together.

"We stuck to the sidewalk, passing block after block of drab, concrete-slabbed high rises. If more than a single human approached from the opposite direction, we stepped out into the street giving deference to them. More than once, a group of young teens sitting on the front steps of decaying apartment buildings caught sight of the odd looking pair that we were and rushed into the street, surrounding us.

"'Just keep walkin,' my partner whispered out of the corner of his mouth at the first sign of their advance. 'Don'tcha slow down and don'tcha try runnin', neither.

"'Whatcha doin' down here in the projects, Whitey? Watcha doin' walkin' beside a honky, bro?' Were always the first two questions.

"'He's a friend of mine,' was always the singular response.

"As we moved on up the block, they would fade back like a pack of dogs chasing a too-fast car, losing interest, only to be replaced shortly by another group.

"And it did almost seem like we were old friends, with a singular purpose—to get the hell out of Dodge, the difference between our escapes being measured only by time. If my luck held out, I hoped to be out in another hour, walking at the pace we were keeping; an hour that secmed like an eternity. It would take him several years at best, I figured.

"His name was Johnny. Turns out he was going to school somewhere downtown. At eleven o'clock at night? Now that's dedication, I thought. During brief periods of quict, before being set upon again, we talked about going to school, about baseball—he'd never been to a major league game, and about being humiliated by others.

Only once did an older group approach us. Most of the time, we were already past the steps where they huddled in drug-addled stupors before recognizing the anomaly that had just past them by. Shouted remarks, few of which I could decipher, would be met with a nod of the head or a wave of the hand from Johnny. But this group of nineteen year-olds saw us coming and flowed swiftly out onto the street to which we'd retreated.

"'Be cool, man,' I heard Johnny say out of earshot of this new threat.

"One of them grabbed my torn shirt sleeve, and it ripped a little more. I kept moving, pushing past them, not uttering a sound, always looking down while Johnny, raising his voice, distracted them into some jive talk about what was going on in the 'hood before inching away from them toward me. As we moved away, I had to remind myself to breath.

"Twice I heard gunshots in the distance, muffled by the high-rises that fronted the street. Other groups loitered in the shadows between buildings by broken-down playground equipment planted in the packed, grass-starved dirt.

"We kept walking side-by-side another two miles until all at once; I could see the bustle of traffic in the distance. There were CTA buses in view and the unmistakable click-clack of the 'El' somewhere ahead. A few more blocks of warehouses and businesses with gated, glass fronts passed by and at last we arrived on a corner with a driverless bus idling by the curb. Johnny said I'd be all right from here on.

We stood there for a minute while I thanked him and of-fered him what money I had left in my blue jeans pocket as a token of my appreciation for what he'd just done. He refused to take it.

There was a tavern on the corner behind us, the front door propped open with a brick to the sultry night air. My ragged shirt was soaked through with sweat. The plate glass win-dows facing the street were painted over. From inside, sounds of laughter wafted out to us. Where we stood on the sidewalk, you could see a television atop a glass-doored cooler at the far end of the wooden bar. It was like looking into a tunnel. All the heads at the bar were turned toward the television, its blue glow reflected off a multitude of surfaces: their blonde or auburn hair, the glistening moisture from sweating mugs, and the gleaming, waxed bar top. A West Coast ballgame had everyone's attention, including the bar-tender who was standing there with his back to us, his mas-sive, tattooed forearm propped against the bar's edge with a white dishtowel draped over his shoulder.

"I offered to buy Johnny a beer, insisting that he join me, that I owed him something. It was the very least I could do for him, I thought. He continued to refuse, offering the time of night as an excuse.

"'Surely, as fast as we walked, you have a few minutes to kill,' I said.

"He glanced in the direction of the open door that looked so inviting to me, and refused again. I turned back toward the open door and tried once more to persuade him.

"'Well, at least come in, sit down, and rest for a minute,' I insisted, thinking, with no disrespect, that he was a teetotaler.

"When I turned back, he was already half way across the street, heading north.

"'Good luck,' I hollered after him. 'Thanks again, man!'

"He waved his hand without looking back and disappeared around the corner where the city bus was parked.

"I walked into the tavern and leaned against the bar, for the first time aware of my rubbery legs, asking where the pay phone was so I could call a cab. I didn't know any of the bus routes or schedules, and, thanks to Johnny, I still had enough money for cab fare.

"The tavern didn't have a pay phone according to the bartender, but he lifted a phone up on to the counter and told me the number to call from memory.

"'Too many miscreants of the wrong complexion came in wanting to use the pay phone, so I had it taken out,' he explained to me for no particular reason. But now I understood Johnny's not wanting to join me.

"Sitting at an otherwise empty table across from the bar, waiting on a cab while I sipped a beer, I took stock of how the night had unfolded, trying to understand where I'd went wrong, wondering maliciously if being a 'smartass' was an inherited trait and, if so, how many new 'Jesse's' would there be in the next score of years.

"Some people, I decided, are addicted to drugs, some to alcohol, some to the belittlement of others, and some, like me, to pride and principles of little value in the real world; each vice as bad as the next. I made a pact with myself, right then and there, to keep them all at bay.

Through scratches in the painted window I glimpsed a cab pulling up to the curb and got up to leave. From now on, compromise would be my new creed. After all, it was just a hat; just a God damned hat."

When Martin finished, a waxing moon had replaced the sun. We looked at him and each other. And I marveled at the changes the past quarter century had wrought.

Rick Elliott

The Oasis

The typical Tuesday night crowd at the Oasis was just that; no crowd at all. Four townies were playing snooker on the back table under the stuffed lion head whose fur glowed blue from of an adjacent Hamm's Beer clock hanging on the wall.

The lion was a trophy the first generation owner of the Oasis had brought back from Africa. He was killed one night not long after his return from the safari, during a robbery here at the pool hall.

Jack, my roommate, was feverishly shooting a flock of robotic geese as they flew in formation across the fake-looking sky of an electronic hunting game attached to the wall at the end of the mirrored bar. Ronnie, a poker buddy of ours and from my hometown, was scraping down the massive grill at the other end of the bar with what looked like an oversized brick, both hands gripping it firmly as he pushed and pulled his way across the massive grill, his soiled white apron rocking to and fro as he scrubbed.

Francis O'Malley, the second-generation owner, was adamant about having the grill cleaned before Friday morning. Friday's and Saturday's were fish days, and the big vat of hot grease would be sitting on that grill all day, both days, while drunken alumni were shoe-horned into the place like sardines.

I was sitting next to Jack, keeping one eye on the geese, hoping he would miss the next shot so I could win. In addition, I followed the college basketball game tuned in on the TV hanging by chains from the stamped tin ceiling, with a watchful glance every now and then back towards the townies.

Jack, ham-fisted and uncoordinated, slammed the control box down on the counter muttering an obscenity under his breath after his last shot failed to score a hit on the two-dimensional Canadians.

"What are you grinning at, pinhead," he snarled.

"I wasn't smiling because you lost," I said, which was half true. "I was smiling about the latest words of wit someone scribbled on men's bathroom wall."

"Oh yeah, was it Shakespearean?"

"No, but it's very apropos for this week's events. Let me quote, 'other than that Mrs. Sadat, how did you like the parade?'"

Jack looked thoughtful as he mouthed the words, thinking, then he let out a snort of laughter while shaking his head. "That's cruel..., but I like it."

"Hey, Ronnie boy," Jack shouted toward the other end of the bar, "are you up to your old habit of writing wits of wisdom on bathroom walls?"

"No, it wasn't me," he said with a broad grin while wiping his hands on his apron as he came toward us. "The 'Etiquette Police' took that guy away just before you two showed up. They said they would be back; so watch yourselves."

We were all smiling now. Ronnie lived in a second floor apartment of an old house that was once a stately mansion. Due to its close proximity to campus, it had been reduced to providing shelter to the likes of Ronnie. He lived with a sometimes girlfriend who was high on etiquette and a vain parakeet that ceaselessly watched itself in the mirror attached to the medicine cabinet in their bathroom.

Ronnie, an English major, was in the habit of writing all kinds of prose on the walls of his apartment bathroom, and it became a ritual for others who visited the apartment to do the same; much to the chagrin of his girlfriend.

Jack and I had penned several notable lines on the wall, and, after a few well-attended parties, the walls were almost covered. A trip to the bathroom became a unique experience as one perused the abstract writings and the parakeet watched himself in the mirror while you did nature's duty.

Who's winning the game?" Ronnie asked as he pulled three cold ones out of the cooler, wiping off the condensation with his gritty apron.

"The Blue Demons are getting crucified by the Saints," Jack quipped.

"Your Religious Studies 101 professor would be proud of you," I chuckled.

We stood there in silence for a few minutes watching the game, the stillness being broken in uneven tones by the sharp crack of balls colliding on the snooker table and our bottles tapping on the polished wooden bar.

Cars swooshed by outside through the drizzle, their lights reflecting in a chaotic array through the plate glass window with "The Oasis, since 1938" painted across it in an arch.

Ronnie began filling the coolers behind the bar with a multitude of beer brands in anticipation of tomorrow's crowd. There were ten cases of bottles stacked on the church pew at the end of the bar beside the first pool table. I had helped him bring them up from the basement in the back of the building. It was the least I could do for the free brews that, on occasion, came my way. We usually paid unless money was tight. Right now, Jack and I were tapped out.

The hair on my neck bristled when a cold draft of air whistled in through the opening front door. Our heads turned in unison toward the door in time to see two angels skipping over the threshold to avoid a deluge of water from a passing panel van spraying a fountain of street water onto the sidewalk outside.

While college girls came into the Oasis often enough so as not to be a novelty, it was clear these two weren't from the university.

They pranced toward our end of the bar, both wearing short skirts with legs up to here. The dark-haired one had what appeared to be a box hanging at her mid-section supported by a three-inch wide leather strap going behind her neck and disappearing under her curly tresses only to reappear and connect to the other side of the tray, like what a vender at a ballgame hawking peanuts would use. Suddenly, I could picture an old TV commercial in my head of a beautiful woman strolling through an elegantly dressed crowd at a party as she asked in a silky voice, "cigar, cigarette, tiparillo?"

Indeed, as the dark-haired one strolled up next to me, I could see the tray she was carrying contained half-sized packets of Camel cigarettes. Her friend, or, perhaps more appropriately, her accomplice, Brandi, asked to speak with the manager.

Ronnie stammered, "He…, he's…, not…, I mean I'm the manager."

Jack and I snorted. Ronnie shot us an evil glance.

"I'm the night manager. What can I help you lovely ladies with?" he asked, with more authority, getting his sea legs under him.

Brandi, the blonde, carried a glitzy leather satchel. She said they represented an advertising agency from Chicago. They were here to give away free samples of cigarettes and other prizes as a promotion, with Ronnie's permission, of course.

She flashed her bright whites at Ronnie in a smile that would have domesticated Attila the Hun. At the same time, her dark-haired twin, Holly, I believe it was—the names no doubt changed from bar to bar—handed each of us a pint-sized packet of Camel cigarettes out of the tray.

"You men look like smokers," she cooed in a sultry voice that made you think indeed you were a smoker, lumberjack, lifeguard and lady's man.

These two were polished like family silver. Whatever ad agency had hired them knew what they were doing. They looked as if they had just stepped out of a display window at Marshall Fields. We, at least I, were putty in their hands.

Ronnie, grounded more in reality than I and with an unsteady girlfriend, spoke up.

"You mentioned prizes, eh?"

He grabbed a toothpick out of the converted Wide Mouth Mickeys' bottle, which was right next to the Corona salt and pepper shakers. This place wasn't called The Oasis for nothing.

"What kind of prizes are we talking about?" He queried, toothpick hanging Brando-style from his lips. "Sex toys, weekend getaways or something more exotic?"

Brandi rolled her eyes and shook her head throwing her glossy hair off her shoulders.

"We have something better. Something that will keep you men warm on a cold night like this," she said with mock lust.

We were all ears…, bulging eyes…, with mouths' agape.

She reached into her fine leather bag and pulled out a wool neck scarf and matching watchman's cap plus a cotton jersey shirt, all with CAMEL emblazoned on them.

"Hey, those shirts are cool," Ronnie cried out child-like, reaching across the bar to grab it.

Brandi playfully slapped at his hand and pulled the shirt away. My mouth closed, inside I was weeping, my lusty daydream crushed. My batting average with girls had been on a downhill slide for months.

"First, we have to have a contest," she exclaimed, wagging a finger at us.

"A contest!" We shouted disbelieving our ears.

"Yes, in order to win the prizes we have to have a contest; orders from our boss," Brandi explained, nodding her head matter-of-factly.

Did I mention her flowing blonde hair?

Jack and Ronnie were becoming annoyed. These two ladies must have thought we were right off the plowed field. They were a third right.

"What kind of a contest?" Ronnie hissed as he slid open the cooler door and went back to loading it to the gills with longneck bottles of beer.

"Let's have a beer chugging contest," Holly chimed in. "It could be a team contest; between you and those fellows at the pool table back there under the lion's head."

The two angels nodded their heads in agreement, a mischievous sparkle in their eyes. They could be in theatre judging from their performance, I mused.

Ronnie, with managerial professionalism, groused.

"What if they don't want to have a beer chugging contest? And by the way it's a *snooker* table" he corrected her, nodding towards the townies. "And who's going to pay for the beer?"

"Oh, we'll spring for the beer," Brandi stated undeterred. "Holly and I will go have a heart-to-heart talk with them."

At first my eyes lit up with the thought of free beer; a conditioned response in any well-schooled college student. Next, jealousy began creeping into my thoughts as I watched them sway to and fro towards the snooker table. What if the townies were wittier than us? What if, God forbid, they beat us in a beer chugging contest? Our manhood was being challenged. Ronnie and Jack didn't look worried. I tried to appear that way. My mind was racing. Beer chugging had never been my forte.

I knew Ronnie from our high school days. He could handle himself around a bottle of beer. Jack, I wasn't so sure about. Other than our midnight Saturday poker games after the Oasis closed, I didn't know his chugging capabilities, though he did have ample stomach capacity.

"You know I never was much of a beer-chugger," I pointed out, trying to let the others down easy.

"Hey buddy boy, I like those shirts," Ronnie confided, pointing at me with one finger, the others gripping the neck of his beer bottle. "And I'm going to get me one of those shirts."

"Yeah, it's time to step up to the plate and be counted, big boy," Jack added.

Leo Durocher couldn't have been more convincing.

Although I was a little concerned with Ronnie's fixation on the shirt; my eyes were fixed on the two cashmere sweaters as the ladies weaved their way around the pool tables back toward us. The townies had put away their cue sticks and were following Holly and Brandi like they were the Pied Piper pluralized.

"Okay!" Brandi announced, "It's all set. They've agreed to a contest with you guys for the prizes."

"Since there're only three of you guys, one of us will be a spectator," the first townie to reach us offered, showing off his math skills. These boys looked hardened.

My suspect chugging abilities still gnawed at me. Ronnie took command, though; his wardrobe needed improving.

"All right, does everyone know the rules for this game?"

Jack and I looked his way, as did the girls and the townies. We congregated around the end of the bar, like managers and umpires huddled around home plate going over the rules before the start of a ballgame.

"What kind of beer are we drinking?" Ronnie barked. "Are we all drinking at the same time and out of bottles or cups?"

One of the townies offered up Budweiser.

Not to look cowed, and because the lovely lasses were from the Windy City, I suggested Old Style; though I'm sure nothing less than fine wine had ever graced their red lips.

Finally, we settled on Busch.

"We can drink faster if we drink out of cups," Jack piped in.

Now, I was beginning to feel better about our chances. It sounded like Jack knew his way around a beer chugging contest.

"Let's have you go single file," Holly chirped. "And, to make sure you drink all of it, you have to place the empty cup upside down on your head before the next person on your team can start."

She had a wry smile on her face, as if she'd just invented sliced bread.

We all thought this scenario over; me especially. Would I look stupider with beer running down my face from cheating; or worse, spewing beer everywhere if I couldn't choke it all down?

In an Oscar-worthy performance, Brandi and Holly were all smiles, beside themselves with glee. The townies looked serious. I looked worried. Ronnie and Jack looked as cool as cucumbers in an ice chest.

"Okay, okay, okay," Brandi shouted, bouncing up and down like a high school cheerleader, "the rules are set. Pour the beer into three glasses per team and set them on the bar. You can decide amongst yourselves who goes first on each team."

Ronnie lined up the glasses and filled them. The three of us crowded together. Ronnie knew I was the weak link. He proposed that I should be in the middle. I didn't argue. I knew he was right as I looked into his eyes and saw the jersey shirts staring back at me.

"Who should go first," I pondered out loud, "Ronnie's a pretty good drinker."

I had to stick up for a hometown lad. Jack, being the gentleman, said he would go first. We nodded in agreement and broke our huddle, determined to win. The townies were ready, too.

"When I say go, the first member of each team will begin," Brandi instructed. "When you're done, put the glass on top of your head, upside down. The first team done gets the scarves, the hats *and* the shirts."

We were all facing the bar. Ronnie was to the right of me. From the mirror behind the bar, I could see the fire in his eyes and a half smile on his face. Jack, to my left, looking toward the floor, collected his thoughts, as he rocked back on his heels. He gripped the glass with his left hand, like a weight lifter ready for the clean and jerk. In a ritual bourn from ancient times we did an about face to look our opponents squarely in the eye.

"Holly," shouted Brandi pointing toward the townies, "You watch those guys, and I'll watch this team. Any cheating or beer running down your face and your team loses, *big time*."

She was a tigress.

"Are you ready?" she asked, looking down the row of six determined, grim-faced competitors. We nodded our heads in unison. "Get set! Go!"

The townies took an early lead as the first one on their team anticipated her command and hoisted the glass to his lips well before Jack. But now Jack was out of the starting gate and with the long stride of a thoroughbred he was pouring down the beer.

Jack, being a college boy, remembered to put the empty glass upside down on his head. The first townie had forgotten for a second before remembering the drill. We were out in front, but now it was my turn.

I raised the glass, tipped my head back and began swallowing as fast as I could. This was my plan; drink or drown. The beer flowed down my gullet like the Niagara during a spring thaw. It was three-quarters gone when I began to want for air. I stopped in mid-swallow, my mouth now filling with beer. All eyes were glued upon me. I snorted air through my nose, and, with one giant gulp, sucked down remainder of the beer.

Now, we were behind. I flipped the glass onto my head as I suppressed a cough. Ronnie never hesitated. I felt pride, plus the beer, swell up in me. I had managed to down the whole glass. More important though, Ronnie was showing what true champions are made of. Everyone, including the townies, was in awe.

If Guinness, the book not the beer, has a record for beer chugging, Ronnie must own it. He put the glass on his head, let out a hearty belch and smiled with satisfaction. The prizes were ours.

The townies were good sports, and we all shook hands before they headed back to the snooker table. Brandi and

Holly gave us our wardrobes. Ronnie took his scarf and playfully lassoed the girls. But with the suave and debonair manner of socialites from the Windy City's north side, they bowed away and gracefully made their exit.

Ronnie took off his apron, put on his prize shirt, and pumped his fist in the air as he spied himself in the mirrored bar.

"Hey!" I shouted toward Ronnie. "Did they pay for the beer?"

He looked at me and frowned. We both knew the answer as we glanced toward the vacant front door. Their little skit had been well-rehearsed.

"Francis will have to pay for these," he said, throwing the empty bottles into their case. "Chalk it up to advertisement."

Spoken like a true night manager, I thought.

I grabbed my tattered book pack from the stained, wooden floor and slung it over my shoulder. Jack decided to stick around to watch the end of the ballgame. I headed for home to study, stepping out the front door and crossing High Street just as a March drizzle morphed into sleet. But with a cap on my head and a wool scarf around my neck, life was good.

I wasn't much of a hat wearer, and the scarf was itchy. But I wore that shirt for years and years. And remnants of that night still remain. While I rarely smoke, it's always Camels. That advertising executive; he was a genius.

Fountains of Youth

Myself? I'm a farmer now. Johnny Simpson, along with his wife Kay, runs a transmission shop over in Toledo. Not very artistic careers you might say, eh? In fact, you might think somewhat boring. Maybe, in Johnny's case, I would agree. Me? I still have my artistic moments, though I've noticed they're beginning to wane. I read somewhere once that the ol' creative juices begin to disappear as you age. Maybe that's the truth of it, because there was a time in our younger lives when our artistic endeavors reached a pinnacle, and our creative juices flowed like a river. I dare say, if I may be so bold, unsurpassed by the likes of Mozart or Monet. No, we weren't composers or painters. At the time, free-form dance was our medium of expression.

The first breakthrough in our creative period came during junior year gym class. Our P.E. teacher, Mr. Pritchett, had other obligations that day so he left us to fend for ourselves. In his absence, we developed slow-motion basketball. It was an epiphany.

None of us were talented enough to mimic the moves in real time of say a Larry Bird or Magic Johnson. I was too short. Johnny was tall enough to dunk, but he couldn't jump high enough to land on a dime. In slow motion though, with a few understudies, we could do all the moves.

Everyone caught on to the flow of the dance routine. I grabbed a step-ladder the janitor had left just inside the locker room door and placed it next to the basket.

We whirled, we pick and rolled. With the grace of a gazelle, one of us would climb the ladder—in slow-motion mind you—for a behind-the-back reverse slam dunk off an alley-oop pass that reached its zenith near the rafters of the old 30's era gymnasium. A beautiful head fake would take two seconds, the pick and rolls at least four.

When we switched to a zone defense, raising our hands in unison, our participants had the look of a choreographed Broadway dance number. In response to our opponent's moves, we slid across the polished wood floor in our Adidas's, first one way, then the other in an undulating wave of humanity. The only sounds were the squeak of our sneakers and an occasional insuppressible laugh.

In addition to their eloquent moves, we tried to show the grimaces and pained expressions on the faces of the superstars we admired as we went diving—slowly—out of bounds to save an errant ball. High fives' were in slow motion, too.

Principal Norden, at the request of our ever wary P.E. teacher, stepped into the gym to check on us. It was our first performance before a live audience.

To our dismay, he wasn't a patron of the fine arts. The concept of slow motion basketball as a dance form was foreign to that medieval cretin. My and Johnny's artistic endeavors would be muffled but only for a little while.

Mr. Pritchett, who was also the varsity basketball coach, got wind of our slow motion game. He thought we were mocking his coaching abilities so for the next week, as a form of punishment, we played bombardment in P.E. class.

Some people might confuse this with dodge ball. That's because they play the sissy version. We used hard rubber balls no bigger than a Christmas orange. With the right velocity and distance, they were known to leave a welt. Coach Pritchett took pleasure in this sadistic game.

He would stand on the stage which ran along one side of the gym watching us from three feet above the out of bounds line. Whistle in hand, with the royal blue stage curtain as a backdrop, he looked like a Roman emperor watching his subjects with relish as they pummeled one another for his personal entertainment.

The far end of the gym had two sets of double doors that led outside to the parking lot. They were chained shut. Isn't that illegal? This was his coliseum and we were his gladiators. No one was going to sneak out. The whistle was for headshots which disqualified you. It must have been broken.

The opposite end of the gymnasium had two heavy, swinging doors. One led down into the men's locker room, the other into the women's. Manhood was gauged by how far the doors would swing inward from the impact of you ball thrown from the center line and meant for someone you disliked.

Bomb or be bombed. It was a simple game. There was no time for artistry here.

Everyone in P.E. class had a nickname, though two in particular stood out. One, Bobby Glasscock, for obvious reasons, was called "Brittle Dick" or "Crystal Balls", depending on the day of the week and whether or not he had a weapon in his hand. He could open the locker room door *all* the way.

The other was Alan Worman. I had taken a disliking to him and always made him my number one target. "Chisel Plow" was his moniker. He talked incessantly about farming in general and Oliver tractors in particular. In any other subject, he made Gomer Pyle look like a genius.

After one tough game of bombardment, having been repeatedly targeted by "Crystal Balls", Johnny and I were soaking our welts in the locker room shower discussing who we had hammered the most. As always, it was the slow-footed "Chisel plow".

The shower room was rectangular in shape, eight feet wide and twenty feet long. A four-inch wide, sloping gutter circumscribed the entire floor along the walls, except at its opening into the rest of the locker room. Showerheads lined all four walls, and, with only one drain in the corner of the cement gutter, the entire floor was perfectly smooth.

Since we weren't paying the hot water bill, everyone left the showers on when exiting which created a sauna; the resulting steam billowing out into the remainder of the locker room gave it an ethereal quality.

On this particular day, the last person to leave the shower—before Johnny and I— spilled an economy-sized bottle of shampoo in the middle of the floor. The cement was slippery before, but now, with the shampoo spreading across it like hot butter, it was like trying to walk on the back of a greased pig.

Attempting to pick up a dropped bar of soap, I fell busting my butt on the hard floor. I writhed in exaggerated agony while Johnny busted a gut watching my theatrics. Then a light bulb turned on in my head.

Like so many great artists, it took pain and personal sacrifice to bring out the genius in me. Still lying on the floor, I pushed off the wall with my feet, gliding effortlessly by Johnny as he watched me speed past with soap suds boiling up in the wake of my path. I was going fast enough that I had to brace myself for impact as I collided with the far wall. An ice hockey rink had more friction than that shower floor.

I recoiled and shot back across the slick cement to the other end. Johnny squirted more shampoo on the floor and joined me.

At first, we raced from one end of the shower to the other, banging into the wall with a thud. On our butts, on our stomachs, on our backs with hands folded behind our heads we floated by the door opening into the locker room.

"Crystal Balls" saw us first, but soon the entire P.E. class gathered around the opening to watch the show. Johnny went flying by once on his side, head resting on his hand with elbow on the floor in repose as if he were sprawled out on the sofa watching a TV show. We began to synchronize our slides so that we crossed the shower opening at the same time going in opposite directions. Our audience was mesmerized.

Sometimes, artistic talent requires a little luck to reach new heights. And as luck would have it, I had a nice gap between my upper front teeth which until now had only made me a good whistler. My parents refused to get me braces; always reasoning that sooner or later I'd get my teeth knocked out and then look at what a waste of money it would have been. A few months later they bought a new Chrysler.

I hesitated at one end of the long, narrow shower with my feet pressed flat against the wall, knees bent. Leaning back, I took in a mouth full of water from the nearest showerhead and pushed off, facing the crowd. As I passed them, I shot a stream of water through my teeth that arched over the audience gathered around to watch this great spectacle unfolding before their eyes.

Johnny was a quick study. We reloaded with water and took off in tandem. Mine a forceful, pinpoint stream while his was more of a spray. He had good teeth.

Back and forth we slid. A dozen heads swayed with each pass of the shower room opening like sea oats on a windy shore, wanting to revel in our latest creation but trying not to get soaked as we glided by; two glistening fountains of youth.

I hollered at Johnny to go by with our eyes closed for added effect. Nothing is too daring for an artist in the throes of a creative stupor. As we crossed by without colliding, water spouting from our mouths, I heard a collective gasp from the audience—like when a trapeze performer spins blindly through the air only to be caught at the last second by their partner. I thought to myself, this crowd appreciates daring new art, even "Chisel Plow".

As we crossed by again, eyes open this time, I discovered an alternative reason for the accolades from our admirers. There, standing in the opening, was Mr. Pritchett our beloved coach. With my deadeye teeth, I'd tattooed a bead of water right across his forehead. Johnny, being less talented, had simply soaked him from the waist down. When we crossed by again, Mr. Pritchett, arm outstretched, water dripping off his aquiline nose, beckoned us with his bony finger to come hither. Not a word was spoken. At once, the appreciative crowd began to recede into the depths of the locker room. Our meteoric rise in the realm of free-form dance was about to be stifled once more.

We were banished from the shower room until the end of the semester. We still had to attend 11:00 P.E. class, though. The rest of our day was to be spent sweaty and smelly. After about a week, Johnny pleaded his case to Principle Norden. Something along the line of having no love life due to his B.O. and that it would warp him into adulthood if he wasn't allowed to shower. He groveled shamelessly.

I was unwilling to yield. To conform to peer pressure about my art was unthinkable. I walked around all semester sweaty, wearing it like a badge except on the few occasions when I sneaked into the locker room shower to practice my moves. Free-form shower dancing was my medium now. I refused to be kowtowed into painting sterile landscapes during Mrs. Krueger's sixth hour art class for the rest of my days.

Even upshot young dancers need down time to rest their weary bones. The concrete walls of that shower were unforgiving. I nursed my bruised body for a few weeks in honor study hall, choreographing in my mind the next great performance.

If you were an upper classman with a B average, you could go to honor study hall instead of the boring, teacher-monitored study hall. I had two classes that raised my average to a B. One, social studies, taught by Mr. Finch, was made easy by the fact that he was a die-hard White Sox fan; an anomaly that made him more foreign than an Ethiopian goat herder in our midst. This was Cardinal-Cub territory. It came with a rivalry strong enough to result in fisticuffs on occasion. Mr. Finch's tests were either fill-in-the-blank or match-the-letter to the correct statement. If the answers were correct, they always spelled C-H-I-C-A-G-O W-H-I-T-E S-O-X.

The other class was Geometry. Math was a subject I was good at but never felt comfortable with. It was made even more uncomfortable for me by Jenny Sanderson. When she sashayed to the blackboard in her short skirt, reaching up high to write the answer to a math problem, wires in my brain short-circuited. Two times two equaled thirteen and quadrangles were five-sided.

Honor study hall was in the basement of the old part of the school that had been built during the depression by the CCC. The basement consisted of three rooms: the cafeteria, a foyer at the bottom of the stairs that contained candy and pop machines and a windowless room we called "the tomb".

The tomb had a ping pong table, four broken down, stuffed chairs, a sofa and a television. The TV got three channels: snow, snowier and snowiest. In addition, there was a radio. With FM stations still in their infancy, all we could pull in was WLS, an AM rock station out of Chicago, two hundred miles to the north.

Most of the girls sat in the brightly-lit cafeteria and studied; an obscure concept for the rest of us who lounged in the tomb discussing politics, sports and the female form, not necessarily in that order.

Politics was a sleeper for us. Watergate had been resolved a few months earlier with Nixon saying a*dios* from the steps of Air Force One. Vietnam was receding into the file cabinet of unpleasant history, although for Johnny and myself, there were a few misplaced files.

I'd lost an older cousin after sixty days "in-country" and Johnny's brother came home with two stubs and a wheel chair. He lasted two years back home before deciding to pack it in for good. Could you blame him? Small town life could be stifling enough with two good legs.

In addition to our discussions, we played ping pong, sang along with the radio and listened for the sound of the candy machine. It was a relic brought over on the Mayflower. After putting your money in (back then it took thirty-five cents), you pulled on one of eight knobs to make your selection. When pulled, the knob and its attached steel shaft extended out four inches with a loud, mechanical-sounding "ker-chunk", then out would drop your candy bar below.

One of my fellow "honor students"—the title falls into question here—discovered that the inner workings of that ancient candy machine didn't always work. Sometimes you could pull on the handle again, and, "kerchunk", out would drop another candy bar without the aid of any money. A rigged slot machine couldn't pay off any better.

Everyone passing by the candy machine on their way to the tomb was conditioned to check those knobs. If those of us in the tomb heard "kerchunk" "kerchunk" not preceded by the rattle of coins descending into the bowels of that machine, silence befell the room, our ears perked and our heads turned like deer caught in headlights. Then, we'd pounce on that machine like a leopard that hadn't had a meal in a week.

Some of our slyer mates would go slower between "kerchunks", rattling a coin in the slot before the next "kerchunk" so as not to arouse our suspicions. Those twits, who did they think they were fooling?

When I got lucky with the machine, being a more honorable honor student, I simply pulled as fast as physically possible—"kerchunk" "kerchunk" "kerchunk"—grabbing every candy bar I could while bracing myself for the savage onslaught from the rest of those slobbering hyenas in the tomb.

One day during P.E. class about a month later, Coach Pritchett instructed us to head outside to the baseball diamond. It was *so* nice out he decided we should play softball to get some fresh air. "Nice" to him was fifty-five degrees and gale force winds, with us in t-shirts and gym shorts while he wore sweat pants and a heavy coat.

It bears mentioning here that the ratty t-shirt I was wearing looked like it had been on the wrong end of a shotgun blast. I'd decided if I wasn't allowed to bathe, why bother with washing or mending my P.E. clothes.

While Coach was retrieving the balls and bats out of the storage building next to the ball diamond, Johnny and I were leaning against the jagged, wire mesh backstop halfway between home plate and third base. We were being subjected to an unsolicited conversation with "Chisel Plow" on the merits of conventional row crop farming versus no-till.

Coach Pritchett hollered at us to get our lazy butts out onto the ball field. At that moment, I spotted a swirling whirlwind as it leaped the low hedge separating the city cemetery from the outfield of the school's ball diamond. It flittered across deep right field, picking up steam, kicking up bits of cut grass and loose dirt as it spirited toward us.

Eureka! A new inspiration came into my head. Without hesitation, I began to pirouette toward the whirlwind, my hands clasped over my head, eyes shut. Unbeknownst to me, my ragged shirt had snagged on the fence, unraveling as I twirled across the infield all the way out past the pitcher's mound where I stopped to catch my breath.

The dust devil swept over me just as I paused. In that moment, nature and art had merged. One single, dingy white, cotton thread billowed between the fence and what was left of my t-shirt some seventy feet apart. My God it was brilliant!

My teammates looked on, mouths agape, in awe at first before joining in, spinning about the ball field haphazardly. They knew I had danced my way to the pinnacle of this art form, and they rejoiced.

Inspired by the event, Johnny looked heavenward. Coach Pritchett's face looked like a shiny new stop sign. I stood there, basking in the glory of my work, glowing in the fusion of man's desire and nature's unrelenting fury.

We spent the rest of P.E. period sitting on the bleachers in the gymnasium, being lectured to by Principle Norden on the topic of taking life seriously while Coach Pritchett sat there, eyes glazed, methodically tapping a ball bat against the side of his head. At least it was warm in there, considering I was wearing only half a t-shirt. But deep down I feared my life as a dancer was drawing nigh. And sure enough, the rest of my P.E. classes were spent under the close tutelage of Principle Norden in his office.

Now, years later, here I am, a farmer, reminiscing about what might have been if my artistic gifts had been encouraged. My regrets are tempered by the degree of freedom I've maintained as I amble across the bean stubble toward the end of the field where I had parked my equipment the night before.

And there it was once more; a giant whirlwind twisting its way toward me across the neighbor's freshly plowed field. Could it be the same one after so many growing seasons? It skipped across the gravel road, and, for a moment, pranced in front of me, tormenting my thoughts of the past. Bits of cornstalks, husks and grey-black soil were swallowed by it, spiraling to its apex, only to lose steam and falter back into the center of the swirling vortex.

Once more I closed my eyes and gave chase, twirling across an eighty acre stage.

In my mind, I could still see that locker room shower scene. Only this time, it was playing out on the second floor of MOMA on 53rd street in New York City. Water vapor from dry ice was rising all around to create the illusion of steam. Theater seating for the patrons looked down into the setting from above. Money-starved, nude dancers from the local performing arts institute took the place of a younger Johnny and me, sliding to and fro in various choreographed positions to earn a few extra bucks during school. Occasionally, by invitation only, when they were in town, guest artists like Baryshnikov, Balanchine, or Raquel Welch would participate in the exhibition. I would drop by, when time permitted, from my flat on the Upper East Side to discuss my latest work and to sign autographs, hiding my balding pate beneath a chic beret.

Out of breath, I stopped and opened my eyes to see it was gone. The whirlwind had frolicked over the horizon and disappeared. Meanwhile, fissures began to appear in the leaden November sky through which shafts of light angled for the earth as I stood there, panting; not regretting the attempt.

I climbed aboard my palette and easel. A couple squirts of ether to appease its cold-nature; then I turned the key. The John Deere tractor fired and came to life. First, white, medicinal-smelling ether smoke followed by rich, black, diesel exhaust. I inhaled with gusto; the fragrance of raw power; one hundred and fifty horses attached to a tandem disk by a three-inch-thick piece of hardened drawbar steel.

With the vibration of the engine coursing through my bones, I sat there, a ringing in my ears from years spent in too close proximity of its thunderous sound.

My practiced eye swept across the virgin canvass, pondering for the moment my next creation. With one arm stretched out straight ahead, fist closed, thumb pointing skyward, I surveyed the dimensions. Should I do a sensual serpentine pattern or the crisp, clean lines of circles and squares in a descending arc?

The behemoth lurched forward as I let out the clutch and throttled up to full power. First, I'll go to the far corner and sign my name.

Rick Elliott

Pete's Pickled Egg Emporium

Mr. Dawson stepped from behind his mahogany desk to shake hands with the potential new client his secretary had just escorted into the office.

"Hello, Mr. Deadrock I presume?"

"Yes, indeed, Pete Deadrock at your service."

They shook hands vigorously.

"I'm Dillard Dawson, executive vice president in charge of commercial loans here at First Federal Metropolitan Bank. We spoke on the phone about a new business loan."

"Thanks for taking the time to see me," Pete replied, still shaking Mr. Dawson's bony hand and wondering what the other two executive vice presidents he'd passed in the hall were in charge of.

Pete was taught early in life that a firm handshake was a must to get ahead in the business world. His diminutive size and ruddy complexion had earned him the label of "fireplug" by those who knew him, though he was not one to be pissed on.

Dillard smiled. "That's what we're here for; to give away money. We print it in the basement. Hah, hah, just kidding, just kidding."

"I believe you know my accountant, John Shoemacher? He's the one who suggested I come to you," Pete said, straight-faced, wiping away Dillard Dawson's smile.

"Yes, John has been a customer of mine for a long time." Mr. Dawson said nodding toward Mr. Shoemacher in recognition. "In fact, he was a customer way back when I worked at United Consumer's Bank, and, come to think of it, even before that when I was at Citizen's State Bank."

John, by nature a quiet man, was busy adjusting his suspenders. He was of an age and shape that rendered a leather belt unworkable.

"Deadrock? That's somewhat of an unusual last name. Do you have any Native American ancestry?"

"None that I know of," Pete answered, looking heavenward and grimacing, the way some men do when trying to think, as if it hurts, or when they are trying to stymie flatulence.

"That's too bad," Mr. Dawson mused, rubbing his bare chin, a habit he had when deep in thought. "There are several low-interest loan programs available for new, minority-owned businesses. I hate to be pessimistic from the beginning, but money for start-up loans is tight right now what with all the turmoil in the financial markets."

"Hmmm, now that I think about it…"

Dillard Dawson interrupted, "Now, don't get me wrong. I'll take a serious look at your plans, but they need to be air-tight; a sure thing…, or the interest rate will be higher."

After twenty years in banking, he had his spiel down.

Pete began again, "I've been told my grandmother was rather promiscuous. Maybe, I have some Native American ancestors I don't know about."

"Uh, Mr. Deadrock, you got your surname from your father. But, still, you might check your family tree."

"Oh yeah, right, right," Pete conceded, sounding disappointed at a missed opportunity. "Well, my great grandfather was born in England so any hanky-panky would have had to happen before then."

"Yes, well let's forget about that idea for the moment," Mr. Dawson said. "Please, have a seat, gentlemen."

He moved back around the massive desk and sat in his executive, leather chair. His secretary, Missy, brought a tray with a pitcher of water and glasses, reminding him, sotto voce, that the auditors would be arriving at noon.

"John tells me you want the money for some type of food business; something to do with deviled eggs?"

"Pickled eggs, Mr. Dawson, pickled eggs," Pete protested as he made a mental note of the deviled egg idea.

He placed his overburdened satchel beside a cushioned chair and sat down next to John.

"I'm sorry, pickled eggs, and please, call me Dill. Tell me, Mr. Deadrock, what makes you think this business will fly?"

"Call me Pete. Have you ever had a pickled egg, Dill?"

"You mean the kind they have in taverns in a glass jar with a pair of tongs, sitting next to a rack of potato chips and Slim Jims?"

"Yes sirree, those exactly," Pete said, perched at the edge of his chair.

"Well, in all honesty, I'd have to say no, I've never had one."

Dill glanced in Pete's direction, wondering if his answer disappointed his client. Many of these potential loan customers could get upset if you burst their "I'm going to get rich" bubble. He tried to let them down easy. To his surprise, Pete seemed undeterred.

"There you go!"

Pete jumped out of his chair and clapped his hands, excitedly pointing a finger at Dill as he spoke.

"There are millions of potential consumers out there just like you." Pete glanced in John's direction. "He'd never eaten one either until I offered to buy him one a couple of months ago at Tiny's Bar."

Dill took note of Pete's enthusiasm; a must to succeed in sales. Pete jerked open his polished satchel and produced a pint-size jar. Floating inside were four plump, reddish-hued eggs.

"Do you like spicy foods, Dill?"

"They don't make a food too daring for my taste buds," Dill boasted.

Though in truth, as a banker, gambling on golf games at the country club and eating jalapeno pepper poppers was about as wild as it got for Dillard Dawson. Still, he felt compelled to be in tune with his customer's way of living; to be able to keep up with them so to speak; to be one of the "guys". He found most people were uncomfortable around bankers same as he was when in the company of lawyers or auditors.

Dill watched as Pete fished around in the jar before corralling one of his prized possessions.

"These are habanero pepper-flavored," Pete explained, handing one of the jiggling, oblong beauties to Dill. Drops of juice from the egg made a sharp contrast on the teal-colored carpet when they met.

"Kind of a Tex-Mex twist on your basic pickled egg," Pete said while scuffing the carpet with his shoe in a futile attempt to make the stain disappear. "Would you care for one, John?"

"No thanks, it'll ruin my lunch."

Pete screwed the lid on the jar and sat back down as Dill took a big bite. The beads of sweat erupting on his forehead were a testament to the level of habanero essence that a pickled egg could absorb.

"Wow!" Dill fumbled for the pitcher of water. Burgundy-colored juice dripped from his pointy chin. "That's one wild ride!" He exclaimed between gulps of water.

Pete grinned, pleased as punch.

"I have twelve flavors available right now for marketing."

Dill, reaching inside his suit jacket, pulled out a handkerchief and wiped his mouth and brow.

"How did you come up with this idea, Pete?" Dill asked, popping a breath mint in his mouth after another long swig of water.

"Well, it's kind of like you described; I mean about the pickled eggs at the bar. I was sitting in Tiny's one evening nursing a brew and staring at Sally Kershaw, the waitress, through an empty pickled egg jar. It's funny how liquid in the jar magnifies everything, isn't it? Anyway, I thought to myself, you never see a full jar of pickled eggs, right? Am I right?" Pete asked again, nodding his head emphatically, trying to coerce the correct answer out of his audience.

Dill looked to John in search of the correct response, but John was staring blankly at the ceiling.

Dill spoke hesitantly, "I suppose so…, but then you don't know how long that jar has been sitting there. I have to admit, one of the reasons I've never tried a pickled egg so far from a jar in a bar is that I figured they'd been there too long."

"See, Dill," Pete confided, scooting his chair closer to Dill's desk, "that's where you're wrong. It's one of the great aspects of pickled eggs; they never go bad. They're pickled! Kind of like a mummy. You never have to worry about your inventory going bad. I mean what other food product can make that claim, huh? Even Budweiser has a born on date, right?"

"Yeah, yeah, I suppose so," Dill answered. He rocked back in his chair while balancing a pencil between his middle fingers. "Tell me, what are some of the other flavors you have?"

"I have bourbon-soaked eggs. They're twenty-proof," Pete stated proudly. "I think they'll go over big in bars and at parties. And one of my personal favorites is the pineapple-pickled egg. We inject pureed pineapple into the egg before putting it into the pickling solution. I think John here likes the bacon-flavored eggs best."

Pete glanced over at John who was nodding his approval.

"Let's see, I also have watermelon, dill, candied, and, of course, all our eggs are kosher. I'm working on a sweet-n-sour egg, but I can't seem to get the flavor mix quite right…, but I will, you can bank on it."

Pete had a determined look on his face, Dill observed. Leaning back further in his chair, Dillard Dawson propped his feet on his desk. He made a sucking sound as he pressed his tongue against his upper teeth, trying to work free a piece of pickled egg stuck there. Would this deal work? He thought about it for a moment and then decided it was time to get down to the nitty-gritty.

"How much money do you think you'll need to get this project up and running over the next couple of months, Pete?"

"Since I'm putting up some of my own money, plus a lot of sweat equity, I think I'll need about four hundred and fifty grand to get it off the ground."

Dill bit his tongue as his jaw clenched. A bit of blood was visible when his mouth opened as he reached once more for his stained, monogramed handkerchief.

"That's a wot of wegs to swell! Isn't it?" He said, pinching the tip of his tongue to staunch the bleeding.

"Not with two places going," Pete shot back, unfazed, his voice rising.

"Two pwaces?"

"Yes, I've already rented an old Chinese diner over on Broadway that closed a couple of months ago. I'm hoping to have a neon sign up in another week or two, but I need more working capital. That's where you come in, Dill."

"A neon sign?"

Dill scrambled to catch up.

"Yeah, it'll say, 'Pete's Pickled Egg Emporium' in red letters with a turquoise background. Those are my favorite colors," Pete beamed.

"Wow! That's a mouthful," Dill observed, regaining his composure with the bleeding stopped.

"The sign is going to flash. That was John's idea."

They glanced in John's direction with different expression on their faces. John had that look on his face that said, "it's beer o'clock".

"I haven't ordered one for the other place. I just signed the rent contract yesterday. It's over on Chestnut Street, three blocks from downtown. I'm going to call it. Are you ready for this? 'House of Pickled Egg'."

Pete was euphoric. Dill, mouth agape, glared at him then at John.

"House of pickled egg, eh? You wanna know what I think about...," Dill growled, grabbing the arms of his chair just as Pete interrupted.

"You see, Dill, I figure if I sell franchises..."

"Franchises!"

Dill's head was spinning, his thoughts were churning, and his gut was burning. Meanwhile, Pete picked up speed.

"Yeah, franchises. People might not like someone else's name on their business. I mean would a guy named Roger want to own a business called 'Joe's Fish and Chips'?

"Hell no! This way, whoever buys a franchise can put their own name in front. It'll be in the contract. So, if say, you bought a franchise, you would be allowed to call it 'Dill's House of Pickled Eggs'".

Pete was in high gear.

"But the flagship store here in town would be 'Pete's Pickled Egg Emporium'. It would be where we first introduce any new flavors."

Dill rocked to and fro in his chair, lips pursed, his fingertips forming a steeple in front of them as his cheeks rhythmically sucked in and out. John was asleep.

"Have you got any idea how the cash flow will work on this operation?" Dill queried, trying to decide if Pete was a genius or delusional.

"John is the accountant. He knows the numbers side better than me. Hey, John, buddy, wake up."

"Huh...? Oh, sorry, I guess I nodded off."

"Stick with me here, John; two more hours and you'll be back at Tiny's. Right now, Dill would like to see the figures you put together for me."

"Okay, well that's part of the reason I fell asleep. I was up all night readjusting the numbers for you since you changed the prices."

Dill narrowed his eyes, scowling at Pete.

Unfazed, Pete explained, "It's no big deal. Yesterday, I came up with the idea of offering two different sizes of pickled eggs. I figured maybe a regular and then a jumbo size for the heartier appetites. That would give customers more choices, more merchandise on the shelf so to speak. Look at how many sizes of soda bottles and cans a grocery store has lining its shelves."

Just then, Pete snapped his fingers and slapped his forehead with the palm of his hand.

"Oh, man, why didn't I think of this before; organic pickled eggs."

The room was quite for a moment as Pete caught his breath while John scooted his chair over by Dill's desk, laying out the computer-generated spread sheets.

If the business sells three hundred eggs a day at an average of $3.75 per egg, depending on a regular or jumbo that would generate a daily gross of $1,125.00 dollars each day with an annual gross of between a quarter and half million dollars. You need to decide how many days a week you're going to be open," John chastised, glancing toward Pete.

"Boys, boys," Dill chuckled, scratching his head. "I don't know, but that sounds like a lot of eggs to hawk on any given day. I mean three hundred eggs!"

"Oh, man, that's nothing," Pete countered. "Why, one night I watched two guys eat a whole jar by themselves at Tiny's, and there are twenty-five eggs in a jar. And I'm not selling your average 'run of the mill' pickled eggs either. No sirree, Dill, I'm selling gourmet pickled eggs. Here, try another flavor."

Pete reached into his satchel and pulled out another sample. The eggs, bright pink, floated lazily in the quart Mason jar. He reached in, trapped one against the side and plucked it out. Once more, juice dripped on the carpet as he handed it to Dill. The spots from the Tex-Mex sample were almost dry.

"These are candied-apple, cinnamon-flavored eggs."

Dill, after refilling his glass with water, leaned over the trash can at the edge of his desk, shielding his tie with his left hand as he prepared to take a bite.

"Hey, these aren't half bad, not bad at all. Once you get past the texture, they're pretty good," Dill mumbled as pink yolk crumbled out from the corners of his mouth.

Pete looked pleased. John cracked a faint smile. Wiping his chin, Dill shook his head slowly, glancing at the numbers in front of him.

"Still..., that's a lot of eggs to sell, week after week, month after month. Did you say you might gross a half a million a year?"

The bank has to loan money to make money, Dill thought. But even in this booming economy and red-hot housing market, a banker has to give due diligence, or at least the appearance of it, to the income and expense projections.

"Dill!" Pete shouted as he leapt from his chair.

Dill, surprised, coughed up a piece of egg, catching it with his hand.

"I can see you're having trouble getting past the idea of them being in a jar at the end of the bar.

"Remember, I'm talking gourmet here," Pete said, stabbing at the air with a pointed finger. "I'm talking about taking the jar out of the bar, putting it in your car and bringing it home to millions of kitchens. I haven't even mentioned the nutritional value or the potential cancer prevention aspects of the pickled egg."

"Cancer...," Dill suppressed another cough, swallowing hard as he finished the egg, "... prevention. How so?"

"Just last month there was an article in the local paper about people who eat lots of pickled foods products having less risk of pancreatic and bladder cancers."

Pete tossed a photocopy of the article onto Dill's desk.

"Hmmm," Dill mused with his eyebrows raised as he perused the article.

"And just think, Dill, every mother knows the nutritional value of an egg, right? When the little tykes come home from school famished, what is she going to give them, a bottle of soda pop and a candy bar? I don't think so. She's going to give them a glass of chocolate milk and a bright green, lime-flavored pickled egg from 'Pete's Pickled Egg Emporium'."

Dill burped. "Excuse me."

The vermillion color was beginning to fade from his tongue as he considered Pete's comment about nutritional value. He had to admit his own little Denise and Donnie were pudgy; cherubs their grandmother affectionately called them. And, well, yes eggs would be better than the chips they always gravitated to once they were home from school.

"Oh, I almost forgot. I'm not only getting the pickled egg out of the bar, I'm putting it on par with the ballpark hot dog."

Dill and John looked at him, puzzled.

"I got the okay from Jeff Dalton, he's in charge of all concession sales at the Springfield Double A Baseball Stadium, to let me put in four vending carts around the stadium to sell pickled eggs. He wanted an awful big cut of the gross sales, but then I thought to myself, what's a $4.00 pickled egg next to a $7.00 bottle of beer? It's a bargain."

Pete's hands were trembling.

"I can just hear it now," he said, before shouting, "pickled eggs...! Get your ice-cold pickled eggs here!"

Dill smiled.

"Well, Pete, you're quite the entrepreneur. It sure looks like you've done your homework in hatching this project. Have you got a supplier for all these eggs you're going to need?"

"Right now, I've got a chicken farmer down in Belle Vista, Arkansas that can supply me with up to a thousand eggs a day. He even offered to put some onion or garlic in the chicken feed saying the eggs would have that flavor in them; imagine that. I'm toying with the idea of a liver an onion egg right now. But just to be on the safe side I bought a little stock in a couple of poultry operations."

"You bought stock in a chicken company?"

"You bet. That way, if eggs get in short supply, I'll have some pull with them to keep my stores going.

"Dill, I'm telling you, if this thing takes off like it should, and I start selling franchises, why the demand for eggs could skyrocket. I thought I would use some of the profits from the pickled egg business to keep buying more shares. Who knows, I might even corner the market someday. Then just think what I'll be able to charge for a jar of pickled eggs."

"Whoa there, Hoss. You're going to need a whale of a marketing plan for those big ideas," Dill said, hoping to throw a little water on the fire.

Pete's diabolical expression was replaced by a broadening grin. He reached into his bottomless satchel and pulled out a crisp, white t-shirt.

"Here you go, Dill. It's a size small, but maybe your kids could wear it. Have you got kids, Dill?"

"Two."

Dill held the t-shirt in front of him as he read the screen-printed logo out loud. "I Got Pickled In Springfield—Pete's Pickled Egg Emporium." It was in a circle surrounding a picture of a tipsy, humpty dumpty-looking egg.

"I've got it in three other colors," Pete offered.

"I like the picture of the dazed pickled egg with her little arms and legs."

"It's a he. And thanks. I thought of it myself. Sally Kershaw drew the egg with its tongue hanging out and its eyes crossed. She did it on a bar napkin. That girl has a lot of talent."

John nodded his head in agreement.

"No doubt," Dill said, still eyeing the shirt. "No doubt about it."

"I've hired a couple of kids and rented a dunking machine for the fair coming up in two weeks. They're going to dress up in egg costumes and give out free samples. I might even try deep-frying a few flavors just for the fair. And the proceeds from the dunking machine I'll donate to charity.

"Here is a color mockup of a billboard I'm having put up, assuming you give me the loan."

Pete unrolled it across Dill's desk.

Dill stood beside his desk, staring down at the ad, rubbing his chin, momentarily at a loss for words.

"That's quite a looker there," Dill said finally as he read the caption. "Don't Tickle Me, Pickle Me."

"That was my idea," John beamed from his chair. "Doesn't Pete look good in an egg suit with a bikini-clad girl hugging him?"

Dill laughed, nodding his head.

Pete countered, "Hey, that girl was Miss October two years ago. She's a local girl, believe it or not. It still cost me an arm and a leg to get her, but I think it will pay off in the long run."

Pete, standing beside Dill, was admiring himself in the picture, satisfied he'd gotten his money's worth.

"A big name model like her will help me sell franchises. Potential buyers will know I mean business, and that I'm not afraid to shell out the big bucks for national advertising. I've got time rented at a recording studio for a television ad. It'll be on a local channel four times a day with just me in front of the camera in my egg suit."

"Hey, maybe you could have a huge pickle jar made out of Plexiglas and swim around in it while looking at the camera asking someone to buy you," John offered.

The three of them stood there, picturing this scenario in their heads.

Pete grabbed John's hand, shaking it as he congratulated him, "John, you are a genius, indeed. You should have been in advertising not accounting."

The intercom buzzed. Dill's secretary reminded him of his noon appointment.

"Mr. Deadrock," Dill sighed, handing the print ad back to Pete, "you've put a lot of thought into this, haven't you?"

"I sure have, but, to get this train rolling down the tracks at full speed, I need more capital. That's where your bank comes in, Dill. I was all set to invest in an internet startup, but this idea popped into my head and I decided to go with it."

"Absolutely," Dill said. "That's why we're here. John, you've gone over all these income and cost numbers for accuracy?"

"Yes, all the costs reflect the current market conditions," John answered, back in accounting mode.

"Well then, gentlemen," Dill offered, escorting Pete and John toward the door, "I'll go over your proposal and present it to the board. I'm confident we can get you some money for this enterprise."

Laughing, Dill continued, "Heck, now that I think about it, the amount you're wanting is chicken feed in comparison to what I just loaned on a strip mall and a housing development. Of course, those are sure things. We'll probably loan you the money but at a higher interest rate. You know the old adage, 'risk versus reward'."

Pete shrugged, "That's not a problem. Thanks again for your time, Dillard; and for my thirteenth flavor."

"How's that? Dill asked with a puzzled expression.

"When you mentioned deviled eggs earlier, it got me to thinking; why, with a little mustard, sugar and mayonnaise injected into the yolk, viola! Pickled deviled eggs."

Dill and John inched toward the door. Pete stopped, searching into the depths of his satchel a final time.

"Here, I almost forgot. These are another flavor I think you'll enjoy since you like a little kick in your eggs."

He pulled out a jar stuffed with six mauve-colored eggs, jiggling in unison like the rattles on an eastern diamondback.

"They're stuffed with Tabasco sauce along with some other secret ingredients. I call this flavor the 'Wajun Cajun'. You'll talk with a lisp after eating one of these babies."

"Thank-you, Mr. Deadrock, I'll savor every one of them."

Pete said goodbye, finishing with the best French accent he could muster, "Bon appetit!" as he closed the door behind him.

Rick Elliott

About the author:

Rick Elliott lives in the Ozark hills of Missouri with his lovely wife, Janice. He is the author of "The Reluctant Martyr", his first novel.

www.ingramcontent.com/pod-product-compliance
Lightning Source LLC
Chambersburg PA
CBHW060121260626
47160CB00005B/1971

* 9 7 8 0 9 8 4 6 0 0 4 1 0 *